# THADITIES
## *and the*
# CLAN

The Wildwoods of First

CAROLYN WYRSCH

**BALBOA.**
PRESS

A DIVISION OF HAY HOUSE

Balboa Press books may be ordered through booksellers or by contacting:

Balboa Press
A Division of Hay House
1663 Liberty Drive
Bloomington, IN 47403
www.balboapress.com.au
1 (877) 407-4847

Because of the dynamic nature of the Internet, any web addresses or
links contained in this book may have changed since publication and
may no longer be valid. The views expressed in this work are solely those
of the author and do not necessarily reflect the views of the publisher,
and the publisher hereby disclaims any responsibility for them.

The author of this book does not dispense medical advice or prescribe
the use of any technique as a form of treatment for physical, emotional,
or medical problems without the advice of a physician, either directly
or indirectly. The intent of the author is only to offer information
of a general nature to help you in your quest for emotional and
spiritual well-being. In the event you use any of the information in
this book for yourself, which is your constitutional right, the author
and the publisher assume no responsibility for your actions.

Print information available on the last page.

ISBN: 978-1-5043-1542-5 (sc)
ISBN: 978-1-5043-1543-2 (e)

Balboa Press rev. date: 11/14/2018

# CONTENTS

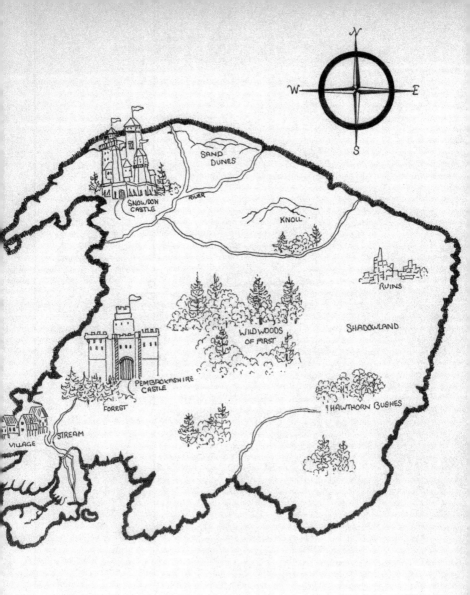

Welddpool

Chapter

# ONE

$O$ak sat up with a start. He found himself in that fuddled state, halfway between dreaming and waking. He recaptured the jubilation he felt when he'd won the quintain tournament. Every squire in the district and beyond had participated in the tussle and he'd won.

His mind had been in a turmoil when he and Flint, a fellow squire, left the main hall, ending one of the most exciting days of his life. Both had returned exhausted to their bed chamber, and without taking off their boots or outer garments, had flopped onto their adjoining cots and fallen into oblivion.

Oak sighed. Was it only yesterday morning that the bailiff had charged into their sleeping chamber and yelled at them to head to the bailey?

He'd shot out of bed and dressed as quickly as his numbed fingers allowed. He'd looked down, and realised his tunic was on back to front. "Not today," he muttered under his breath, while he adjusted his tunic. He bolted out of the chamber and banged into an immovable mass of squires as they all tried to descend the stairs. After untangling his arms and legs he rushed headlong down the dark and narrow steps, trying not to step on anybody's toes. He emerged unscathed into an alien-looking bailey and went and stood next to Flint.

He had reputation of being a tough squire, but the cold was unbearable that morning, as it snaked around his body and froze him to the bone.

It was eerily silent as the thick mist shrouded the castle's landmarks. Oak heard muffled noises coming from over near the drawbridge, and as his eyes adjusted to the gloom, he noticed many dark, ghostly shapes. The mist lightened, and those dark shapes metamorphosed into knights and their squires. They stomped their feet and flung their arms around as they tried to keep warm. Oak thought the noise was deafening.

"Do you recognise any of the banners?" he asked Flint, raising his voice above the clamour.

"Yes, some are local standards," replied Flint.

Oak slowly stiffened as the knights regarded them intently, as if sizing up an opponent. "Oh please," he whispered fervently to himself, "don't let these knights be on the hunt for new squires." He squirmed under their gaze, and to his shame, the dreaded blush crept over his face and down his neck, leaving his skin stained a bright red. He knew he looked more like a serving girl than a knight-in-training. Someone sniggered, but he hoped he'd escaped too much scrutiny from the visitors.

Oak was tall, and with his long, dark unruly curls, piercing green eyes and fair skin, he was always being noticed. His perceived handsomeness had been a point of interest to many of the maids and they were always giggling as he went past.

At the beginning of his training, he'd found it difficult to be taken seriously. He felt fortunate to be apprenticed to Sir Glyneath. His master was tough but fair, and under his tutelage Oak was now an excellent horseman. His strenuous regime with the lance and sword, practised over the last few months, had prepared him well for today's tournament.

Sir Glyneath caught his eye and glared. Then his gaze shifted, as if one of the knights had claimed his attention.

What a horrible start to a feast day, Oak thought.

The knights moved as one, and as they crossed the bailey Oak noted that knights in full armour were a terrifying sight. Their sabatons banged into the cobbles and the loud creaks and clangs that emitted from their armour echoed throughout the bailey and then bounced off the castle walls.

They stopped in front of Oak and many shouted, "Where's the great hall, lad?" They wanted food and ale, they said. They were hungry and thirsty from their long journey. Oak was so relieved that all they required was food and not new squires that he nearly collapsed with relief. He pointed them in the right direction.

"Yes, Sir Glyneath?" Oak enquired, as his master appeared at his side.

His master frowned at him. "Oak, the squires need to be shown the kitchens. Have you checked you armour and weapons?"

"Yes, Sir Glyneath," replied Oak. "It's all ready for the tournament."

Sir Glyneath dipped his head and whispered, "Come closer, Oak."

Oak leaned into Sir Glyneath's skittish horse and gave his full attention to his master. "Listen, lad. You are strong and courageous, and one of the best horsemen around."

Oak was gratified to hear this, but he knew more was coming.

"Therefore, I expect these qualities to be displayed, in abundance, during this afternoon's tournament," Sir Glyneath said. "I have wagered a huge sum of gold on you being the last squire standing. Make sure you don't disappoint me."

Oak stepped to the side of Sir Glyneath's prancing horse and replied, "I am honoured to be chosen as first squire today and to represent you on the King's feast day, sir."

"Do not disappoint me," exhorted Sir Glyneath again. "Now, be off with you to the kitchens."

Chapter

# TWO

Oak and his fellow squires smelt the tantalizing whiff of fresh bread as they clattered into the main kitchen. Pushing to the front of the line, Oak grasped a hand loaf as it came out of the hot oven and roared, "hot," as he juggled it. He covered it with dripping and rammed it into his mouth before the chef could snatch it out of his hands.

"That hurt," he yelled through his mouthful, as he received a clip around the ear for his troubles.

"Good," the chef said.

The sun was just peeping around the edges of the doorway when the squires licked their fingers for a final time. They gave thanks to the chef for breakfast, then they left the kitchen and made their way across the bailey with full stomachs and nervous minds.

Oak's boots skidded on the wet cobbles and he nearly slipped, recovering himself just in time.

"Help," shouted one of the squires, as, less lucky than Oak, he hit the cobbles with a thump.

Oak stopped and pulled him upright.

Thump went another, and brought someone else down with him.

"Watch out," Oak screamed, but it was too late. They all found themselves sprawled on the wet cobbles.

One by one they righted themselves and laughed at their clumsiness as they made their way out of the castle and onto the tournament field.

"Have you finished the armoury check?" Flint asked.

"Yes." Oak shoved a well-polished breast plate under Flint's gaze.

Flint laughed. "After such diligent polishing, Sir Glyneath could just dazzle his opponents until they yield."

As they pulled on their flasks to slake their thirst, Sir Glyneath appeared at the pavilion entrance. He nodded and waited impatiently to be dressed in his armour. It took some time, and Oak was just about finished when they heard the thundering of hundreds of horses' hooves, getting louder and louder as they approached the field.

Sir Glyneath clanged out of the pavilion and Oak helped him onto his horse.

Oak and Flint hopped from one foot to another in great anticipation as they watched the spectacle of the tournament knights. They poured into the field and started parading around like peacocks. Each had a distinct war cry that could be heard for miles. It must have nearly deafened the hundreds of spectators that had the misfortune to be standing in front of them, because Oak and Flint heard the war cries from where they stood, hundreds of yards away.

The knights glanced around with disdain, and then they rode to their allotted pavilions, each recognised by their flying standards. The pavilions had been erected following the ancient rules which saw visiting knights on one side of the field and the local knights on the opposite side.

Oak heard the herald's cry; the cheval tournament was underway. He saw Sir Glyneath as he waited patiently behind his designated line with the bright sun reflecting off his breastplate. Each knight sat astride his horse. They looked like an illustration of battle-hardened warriors going to war.

"One day, that will be us," Oak said.

A braying cry resounded and Sir Glyneath and his fellow knights boldly rode out. With lowered lances pointed to strike their opponents' shields, they dug their heels into their horses' sides and demanded a quickened pace. The horses answered, their hooves banged into the ground and they raced across the open space and met the opposing knights as they cannoned towards them from the opposite side.

Lances struck lances, and many shattered into shards of broken dreams, as each knight tried to carve out a lustrous name for himself.

Oak and Flint watched the knights battle it out for supremacy. It was noisy, bloody, and ferocious; the smell of death was close. There were many injured knights being carried from the field by their servants and squires. Both sides turned, a depleted line reformed and charged again for glory. This age-old pattern was repeated many times that day.

As the sun started dipping in the sky, a handful of knights was left on the field. Sir Glyneath was sitting astride his horse, lance lowered, emitting an excitement that Oak could see palpitating in the air all around him. He rode towards a knight who had been thrown by his horse, hit his shield and knocked the knight to the ground. The knight went down on his knees and begged for mercy. As this was the last knight left on the field, Sir Glyneath was dubbed the winner.

The King shouted, "Sir Glyneath, congratulations. You will be well rewarded at this evening's feast."

Sir Glyneath bowed his head in acknowledgement and headed towards the pavilion. Oak and Flint gave their heartfelt congratulations and helped Sir Glyneath out of his armour before they got ready for their own tournament.

"Don't forget our talk this morning, Oak," said Sir Glyneath.

On arrival at their appointed places, Oak found Flint was second and he third in line. He sat down by his horse and watched the first squire approach the quintain and throw his lance. He missed.

Flint was next and Oak saw Flint was not properly positioned on his horse. He would not be able to tilt effectively. Sure enough, he missed and received a dong on his head from the quintain arm. Oak heard his cry and raised his arm in salute.

Oak mounted his horse and faced the quintain with his lance held firmly in his right hand. He glared at the heart of the shield and charged. The ancient rhythm of movement connected Oak with his beloved horse. It steadied his mind and with an unerring eye, he hammered the lance right into its centre. He ducked his head as the quintain's arm swung his way and then rode back and joined Flint. He dismounted from his horse and smiled.

He sat and watched the other squires. Some hit the shield but forgot to duck the arm and were unseated from their horses. Others missed the shield and received a nasty bang on their heads.

To win when the King was in attendance would boost his reputation and his liege lord would win a pile of gold, thought Oak. Many of the visiting squires sat on the grass with him and Flint, breaking bread and drinking ale and pretending a friendship that did not exist.

At last the line of squires had all taken their turns and Oak had won. He was proud of his mastery of the quintain and pleased he hadn't let his master down.

He and Flint were not expected to help clear the tournament field, only to look after Sir Glyneath's armour, weapons and standard. They completed these tasks with good grace and then they both received an invitation to attend the feast. Since Sir Glyneath was in a good mood, Oak was going to ask for a steel sword to replace the wooden one he now carried.

Strike while the iron's hot. That was his new motto.

When Oak and Flint finally sat down at the end of the large table to join the feast, they were famished. They had served Sir Glyneath all evening and the food had been plentiful and of good quality, because the King loved his food. The King, Oak's Lord and Lady, and their many attendants and guests, including Sir Glyneath, had been seated at the top table. They had eaten pig, wild boar, mutton and lamb. There had been a selection of wild birds and fish, and everything was cooked in herbs and spices. Dishes of vegetables, pies and sauces and beautiful desserts had followed. Wine, ale and water flowed and most of the invited guests were now drunk and flagging at the table.

The King had presented Sir Glyneath with gold coins for being the last knight standing. Oak hadn't caught the name of the last defeated knight, and he was just too tired to care.

Now finally able to take their own meal, Oak and Flint shoved the food down their throats and drank huge draughts of ale. Both soon finished and then they sat around and waited for Sir Glyneath.

As that day crossed into another, the Lord, Lady and the King left the hall and Sir Glyneath finally rose from the top table.

"Go to bed lads," he said to Oak and Flint. He added that he was well pleased with his success today, and that he would be up for hours yet. He would come and find Oak when he wanted to go to bed. "Sleep until then," he told them.

The boys stumbled from the hall and helped one another up the stairs to their quarters.

Chapter

# THREE

Oak woke with a start. Daylight flooded in through the half-open shutters.

He was alone. Silence emanated from the castle walls. Oak glanced over to Flint's cot, but it was empty. He rolled off his own and stumbled from the bedchamber.

"Hello?" he called. Hundreds of people lived in the castle. It was at least mid-morning. The place should be abuzz with conversation, rattles, footfalls and shouts of laughter. Instead, silence reigned.

Was everyone hidden? Was it a jest?' Terrified, he stumbled from room to room. Each was empty.

When he entered the silent bailey, he bolted over the cobbles and checked the great hall; also empty. He ran to the kitchens, and called down the staircase, "Is anybody there?"

Silence. He looked for his Lord and Lady in the castle keep, but it was empty. All the gatehouses and guardrooms were empty. No kinsmen were evident. The livestock were gone. Even his beloved horse had vanished from its stall.

"Sir Glyneath!" Oak wailed, "where are you?"

His fear had increased to fever pitch, and as tears streamed down his face, he gulped for air and realised he was caving in to terror.

The castle was empty. He had not lost his mind.

He stopped and took more deep breaths and decided; one more search to be sure. While he rechecked his bedchamber and the kitchens, he quickly collected a few meagre belongings, food and water. The choice of swords from the armoury took a lot longer. These he tied onto his back. He tucked a steel sword in his belt and with his trusty lance, he walked towards the drawbridge. He stood and looked back into the bailey.

The castle was empty, silent and dead. There was nothing to be gained from staying, so Oak crossed the bridge, turned east towards the sun and hoped he would find some answers at the next village.

As he walked along the familiar route, Oak noticed a build-up of trees on either side of the pathway and he was soon surprised to find himself in a dark and sinister woods. The path was flecked with shards of cold light that seemed to have descended from the limbs of the trees. There were thousands of pine needles scattered around the ground and mounds of these had encroached onto the pathway. The path was also full of holes and littered with sharp stones and twigs. He found it increasingly difficult to walk.

He looked up and noticed the trees were straight and tall, and their canopies were melded together overhead. They stared back with a malevolence that chilled him to his bones. There were so many crammed together they made him feel as small and insignificant as an insect. Fear settled in the pit of his stomach, and he wanted to be sick.

The wood was ominously silent; there was no birdsong, no sound of scurrying animals in the undergrowth, and not so much as an ant in sight. Silence surrounded him.

He felt abandoned and afraid. Perhaps he should have stayed at the castle after all?

His eyes slewed from side to side as he walked, and his mind was alert for any changes to the menacing trees. A wind started to blow through the canopies. An eerie, moaning sound penetrated his ears and he nearly stumbled over a tree root. The wind calmed, the moaning gave way to a gentle whistle and Oak was comforted. He welcomed the breeze; until then the terrible silence had been heavy with menace, and he had not dealt with it very well. Now, the air seemed friendlier somehow...

He looked around and saw only a few straggly trees left at the edges of the pathway. The path in front was now full of welcoming sunlight. He breathed deeply, repositioned his load and turned his face towards the golden orb.

The blazing afternoon sun beat down and burnt his fair skin. His homespun shirt clung to his back and his shallow breath caught in his swollen throat. His skin felt hot.

"Ouch," he yelled, as a sharp pain pierced his skull and brought him to his knees, adding to his misery. Fed up and tired, Oak felt an overwhelming lethargy overtaking him. He crawled under a canopy of branches at the side of the path, took a deep draught of water and stealthily, his eyes closed.

Chapter

# FOUR

$O$ak woke with a fright. He found himself in that fuddled state, halfway between dreaming and waking. He recaptured the jubilation he felt when he'd won the quintain tournament. Every squire in the district and beyond had participated in the tussle and he'd won.

And then... his blurry eyes tried to focus on the green face that glared down at him.

He recalled the First Rule: show no fear. Then he recalled the Second Rule: show no fear.

The green giant closed in and snuffled at his face.

No, not a giant; it wasn't right or a giant.

It was a green dragon.

Oak blinked. He closed his eyes and cringed away. Show no fear. Then he opened his eyes again.

The scene before him was real.

There really was a dragon.

He rose, but a numbness overtook his limbs and clouded his mind, and he found he couldn't move. Moisture ran down his legs, and still the dragon moved closer and he couldn't move.

"Are you a knight?" enquired the green dragon in a rusty roaring voice. Oak perceived it was old.

Other dragons shuffled into view, closer and closer, as if his answer was important.

"Er, yes...sorry, no. I'm a knight-in-training," he mumbled.

He felt the dreaded blush cover his face. He slewed his eyes away from the old dragon and looked down at the uneven ground, and all the time he rubbed his sweaty palms down his wet trousers.

"Oh!" A strangled wail of disbelief emitted from the dragon's elongated, wrinkled green neck.

"What is it?" faltered Oak.

"Our flight has been long, and dangerous and we are exhausted," the green dragon said.

"We waited and waited for hours for two great knights, and we thought we had found them," another said.

"And now you say you're not one of them," a third took up the plaint.

"Have you met many great knights?" Oak asked politely. He recalled all the hours of boring lessons in etiquette he had endured while at court. He was never impolite, even to dragons. Or maybe, especially not to dragons.

The old dragon looked at him with a hard stare, piercing his thin veneer of courage.

"No. We have never met a great knight before. Edgar, our ancient owl seer has foretold that two great knights would be waiting, near the fork of the twin streams. We are in desperate peril and we need these great knights to help defend our lands and villages and find our vanished kinsfolk," the old dragon continued.

Oak now knew this request was getting beyond the realms of reality and had drifted further into the realms of fairy tales.

"Dragons have villages?" he queried. Oak could not imagine such a humongous village.

"Yes," the dragon said. "We live in caves overhanging the sacred cliffs that look out towards an ocean named Y Ddraig Goch. This ocean is dedicated to a fierce warrior, the Red Dragon, a legend who is revered by all. We have lived there peacefully for thousands of years due to his courageous legacy."

"Until now," yelled one of the group.

"Yes, until now," the others chorused, with bowed heads.

Oak craned his neck, looked directly at the elderly dragon, and sought more signs of jesting. The old dragon's sad face showed only confusion.

Oak had had enough of jests.

His heartbeat returned to a steadier rhythm, and then he smelt a disgusting whiff coming off the elderly dragon. It was so overpowering he took an involuntary step backwards. One of the other dragons had stomped over to him, causing the ground to groan, and Oak scuttled closer.

"What are you called?" the old dragon bellowed, as other dragon heads turned and listened to his reply.

With all the courage he could muster, Oak wiped his hands down his damp pants and blurted, "I am Oak, soon to be one of the great knights of the kingdom. What should I call you?" he added with a quaver in his voice. He had never seen a live dragon before. He had only ever seen the image of dragons worked into a tapestry which hung in the castle keep. "Do you have a class system? Are you their leader?"

The elderly dragon drew closer to Oak and said, "I am Chalice, elder and temporary leader of this clan."

Chalice then launched into the myths she'd been told as a young dragon. She had no personal knowledge of knights, she admitted. There were many tales and fabricated stories, handed down through generations, about great knights and courageous dragons who stood together, side by side in battle. But there had also been dark tales, of fearsome dragons that had been demonized by men, and these men called themselves the Dark Knights.

Suddenly, she reared up and shook from head to tail. The ground thundered all around, as words spewed from her mouth. "Now young Oak, our caves are destroyed, and all of our young dragons have disappeared." Chalice's voice shook with anger. "We arrived here today, and we expected to find those who could help us. Now what are we to do? We do not know our enemy!" she cried.

"Chalice…" Oak looked into her eyes, as he called her name. 'There were no great knights waiting at this tree. Just me, all alone. Would I do?'

Chalice looked down at Oak and said, "You will have to do, Oak. There is nobody else."

He gathered his things and asked where they were going.

"Keep up and follow us," Chalice said.

The dragons set off and Oak ran as fast as he could, trying to keep up as they disappeared into an adjoining field where they settled down out of sight of the path. He was breathless by the time he found them, so he unfolded his blanket, found a spot close to a hedge and lay down. He kept one eye open throughout the night, but the dragons just slept and snored.

In the morning, the dragons all shuffled to form a circle and stood around making the most dreadful racket and ignoring him. They left Chalice behind and went and stood in a straight line and tried to outdo each other with their flame-throwing antics, and then their booming laughter rang out, hit the top of the mountains, and bounced back causing further hilarity.

Are they all mad? thought Oak. Maybe they'd all escaped from a mental house and needed to flee their homeland. They behaved like undisciplined children.

"Chalice, what are the other dragons doing?" Oak asked, in a shaky voice. He had watched their daft antics for long enough, and now he wanted to know what they were doing and why the dragons were ignoring both of them.

He turned, and the wind caught his words and send them soaring into the sky. Chalice had moved a short distance away where she spoke to a fierce-looking dragon; one Oak had not seen before.

Oak's ears pricked up when he heard his name. He tilted his head and tried to catch any stray words. He'd slept with one eye open all night and felt exhausted. His heartbeat quickened in his chest, perspiration ran down his back and his legs turned to jelly. Now what?

Chalice returned, with the fierce dragon in tow. The dragon was wearing a dull metal headdress and breast plate, set with beautiful stones. Oak's cautious eyes locked with the dragon's, and looked for signs of hostility, but saw only pity reflected there. His legs gave way, and he toppled over, and crumpled into the dirt. Pain shot through his body, and embarrassed tears seeped from under his eyelids. He took a few minutes to marshal his thoughts, for he felt defeated.

With measured caution, he got to his feet, and was appalled to see the aged dragons had gathered around him in a circle and peered down in bafflement. He opened his mouth to speak, but Chalice pinned him with a hard stare, and said to those assembled, "My knowledge of men and their peculiar behaviour is limited. I would put Oak's display down to nerves and not to bad manners."

"Oak," Chalice called, as the intimidating dragon stepped into the circle. "You have not yet met Thadities. He is our head warrior."

Oak looked at Thadities and then at the aged dragons standing around him and wondered about this quest Chalice had been prattling on about. He would have thought a quest was fought with fierce and bold warriors and not with these aged, saggy, baggy, green dragons. A collection of aged dragons didn't inspire him, a fourteen-year-old knight-in-training, who had won the quintain tournament. He had a sword to prove it, and the dragons needn't know he had just helped himself from the castle's armoury when he woke to find the castle deserted.

Most of the clan peered down at him through eyewear and some had ear trumpets pressed up to their eardrums as they tried to follow the conversation. Oak was further flummoxed when he realised they were wearing coloured shawls around their necks.

Some dangerous clan, Oak thought.

Oak looked Thadities in the eye, and asked, "Where are all the warrior dragons?" He thought a quest required fighting dragons and not these ancient relics. Unwisely, he said so.

Thadities glared at him. "These aged and retired dragons were the trailblazers for most of their lives. Just because their bodies are aged it doesn't mean their brains are dead. They are as sharp as I, when it comes to working out battle strategies. They studied maps, unravelled many codes and are masters at weaving unfathomable plots. They know how to fight with or without fire, with cunning and stealth. Their knowledge of old battles is formidable and their access to facts and ancient ways is stored and kept intact in their brains. Please don't be rude in front of my elders, young Oak."

"But where'd they come from?" Oak asked Thadities.

"I returned to my homeland from a reconnaissance flight and found all my kinsfolk had disappeared. These dragons," he said as he pointed to the clan, "had been on a day trip with their retirement home, and on their return they discovered all their kinsfolk had vanished. They, and I, were the only ones left.

"Chalice retrieved one of Owl's ancient books from the cave and read the notes that he had scribbled in the margin. He wrote about mythical knights who had helped our ancient kinsfolk win great battles, and that one day, we would seek descendants of these great knights when our homeland was threatened by unseen foes. These knights would be found near the fork of the twin streams on a homeland called Welddpool, and they would fight alongside the dragons."

Fight what? Fight who? wondered Oak, but Thadities was focused on calling each of the elders forward to be formally introduced.

"Chalice, you have met. She was our leader, a formidable adversary and a wonderful confidant to all.

"Daphadilly oversaw the armoury. Young dragons returned every piece of armour they borrowed, otherwise their guardians were informed of their transgression.

"Steffen was our code breaker. His mastery of the subject was legendary, and he has never retired.

"Grumpy was an old battle axe; fearless in his time, and even today his knowledge of fighting strategies is still being used.

"Waddle..." Thadities smiled as he introduced the last of the clan. "She looked after the daily needs of the clan, made sure camp was ready for habitation, and settled any disputes between the dragons over domestic matters."

Oak had never heard of anything so ridiculous.

Thadities continued, "And I am a warrior and scout. When I had returned to my homeland, I joined with these elders and attempted to unravel the mystery of why my kinsfolk had vanished. There were no obvious reasons, but Chalice wanted me to honour the old seers' predictions, so we abandoned our homeland and landed on Welddpool, to be told the mythical knights that we'd sought weren't here...but only you."

Thadities sounded unimpressed, and now Oak was worried. How was he going to fit into this tight and odd clan? He was small, fragile and a squire, not a knight. He didn't even come up to the dragons' knees. Even when Oak spoke, they all had to bend down to catch his words. Or, they could have swung him up onto their backs, and he could shout into their ear trumpets. Now, that would be funny.

When they stood in a circle, and peered down at him, he felt so small. Not frightened, just small and insignificant as an ant.

As night devoured the day, casting ghastly shadows from the dragons' bodies, Oak was paralysed with dread. Thadities nudged him with his talon and beckoned him to sleep under his wing. Oak slept through the night despite the overpowering odour.

Chapter

# FIVE

Oak bounced around the clearing the next morning and shouted to the dragons, "Good morning, good morning."

"What did you say lad?" Chalice bellowed. "Your voice needs to be projected farther, otherwise how can you be heard in a middle of a battle?"

"I have practised with Sir Glyneath during battles, but I am not experienced with ear trumpets," Oak shouted, as he focused on her clouded eyes.

While he held her gaze his intuition kicked in and he saw the air around Chalice's mouth shimmer. She hiccupped and out belched a ribbon of fire.

He dived and hit the ground, hard. She missed, but his tunic was singed.

Oak yelled indignantly, "What happened?"

She laughed and called down, "Sorry Oak, my throat needed to be balanced. Thadities has asked me to recall one particular ancient strategy and as I juggled my thoughts my throat control slipped somewhat." Chalice folded her wings close to her body and closed her eyes. "We shall continue our talk later. I am very tired."

Oak rushed over to speak to Thadities.

"Thadities," he shouted, and his voice quivered with indignation. "Chalice singed my tunic and nearly burnt me to death, and then she went to sleep."

Thadities turned and looked at him. He growled, "Oak, childishness will not be tolerated while you are a warrior in our clan. How are you going to live amongst your fellow warriors when you tell tales behind their backs?"

The blush crept over his face, and he hung his head in shame.

After a time, Chalice woke and re-joined the clan. "Time to leave Welddpool and return home," she said. "Thadities, Oak will ride with you and you are rear guard this flight. We're leaving."

The warrior dragon inclined his head and turned to go.

"Oak, follow Thadities," Chalice shouted. "Don't forget to hold on."

Oak trudged behind Thadities and dragged his tattered feelings around him like a well-worn cloak. He was now to be known as a gossip. He would have to watch his tongue.

Thadities stopped beyond the edge of the field and planted his feet hard into the ground. "Time now, Oak," he said in an authoritative voice. "Climb aboard and we will head for the black hole and home."

Taking a deep breath Oak found a raised bump and started to climb. Under his hands, Thadities' skin was leathery, and scattered with bumps.

Oak heaved himself upwards, and secured one hand over a bump, and clung on. He slid his foot sideways and inched towards another bump. He planted his foot with trepidation, and looked for the next hold, which wasn't there. His hand dangled in the air. Oak slammed into Thadities' body and knocked the breath out of his lungs.

Suddenly, a large set of teeth plucked Oak from his predicament, flung him through the air, and before he could call out, dropped him on his bottom, with a resounding thump. Thadities gave him a hard stare, and without a word, swung his head around. Oak found himself seated between the dragon's wings, in a small indentation. He felt a fool.

Oak waited for the next move and noticed Thadities' armour was tarnished and discoloured. "Why is your metal dull and dirty? he asked. "Armour should be polished until it shines."

Thadities replied, "I am a warrior and scout. One of my duties involves flying reconnaissance. I have flown many missions and have never been detected. My bravery and stealth are legendary. Ewloe, my liege lord, is owed a certain number of days every year when he requires me to fight or help with guard duty. The rest of the time is my own, and I have carved out a lucrative career. Why would I alert my enemies to his position by having polished armour?" Thadities flexed his wings before Oak could respond.

Scrabbling around for something to hold onto, he found the breast plate, and slipped his fingers underneath. Clamping his knees tightly, he leaned forward, scared but exhilarated.

The air around him jumped into life, as many wings beat in time, and then streamed towards the horizon. He saw flattened grass and trees bending in every direction, as he and Thadities soared into the sky and joined them.

"Thadities, can you hear me?" Oak screamed. The fear in his voice only frightened him more. "Thadities, please...please answer me."

Silence.

He shoved his fingers farther under the breast plate and shifted his numb bottom a little deeper into the indent. Why had he said to Chalice, 'Would I do?' He had been an eager fool.

There was a sudden shift in the air and Thadities' silhouette was less defined. Oak's stomach sank to his toes and he redoubled his efforts to hold on. The hard metal dug into his fingers, cutting through his flesh, and found the underlying bone. Fascinated, he watched his life blood seep over his hands and disappear into the storm. The pain flashed up his arm and blanked out his mind.

Darkness descended in thick waves, and obliterated Thadities. A zig zag of sharp, white light split the blackness, as lightning bolts cracked across the sky and brought into relief ghostly outlines of the lead dragons, as they hung suspended in the air. Thunder rolled around his head. He was disorientated and in terrible pain.

The storm intensified and brought torrential rain in its wake. "One, two, three," he shouted, as he tried to steady his shattered nerves. Oak inhaled an odour that smelt like thousands of rotten eggs. It was coming off Thadities' wet skin. Gagging, he vomited all over himself and Thadities. He wet himself again and thought it wasn't a glorious start to their quest.

"Thadities," Oak cried when he could speak. His fingers slipped from under the breast plate and terror moved in. The savagery of the rain hampered his hands as they skimmed over Thadities' skin looking for his anchor. He peered into the darkness and looked for the outline of the plate and all he found was a merciless adversary. Fear shot up his spine and he started to shake so hard he slipped even farther forward. His arms flailed, his rubbery legs went from under him and he shot forward.

"Ouch," he yelled, as he slammed into Thadities' bony spine. He scrabbled around with his damaged fingers, but he slipped even more and cannoned straight into the storm.

Hurtling towards his death, Oak's thoughts were jumbled, but being terrified fought for first place. He thought he might go mad, and luckily for him, they were his last coherent thoughts.

"Ouch!" he howled, as Thadities' teeth grazed his chest. His shirt was snagged in the dragon's teeth and Oak was terrified.

Swinging back and forth through the sky brought back memories of a quintain pole. He was unceremoniously dumped onto the indent between Thadities' shoulders. Thadities glared at him with orange glowing eyes that lighted the area until Oak found the edge of the breast plate with his cold and bloodless fingers.

Oak took deep breaths and closed his eyes. The tears slipped unnoticed down his face and disappeared into the rain. He sniffed into his soaked sleeve and he nearly splintered into a thousand pieces. Death had knocked, Thadities had answered, and Oak's life was spared. Why?

Thadities looked as if he was suspended in the sky, then he dipped the tips of his wings and slipped into his position of rear guard. Thadities called and the air thundered all around him as the dragons replied. The dragons were snorting and beating their wings into the pelting rain and sounded like massed drums. Oak was too frighted to slip his hands from under the breast plate to cover his ears, so now he had a sore head to add to his list of horrors.

A row of eyes glowed through a wavering curtain of rain. He wondered if there was more than a physical connection between these dragons. He wanted to know. He had much to learn about these ancient beasts.

Oak shook from head to toe, and his head seemed to have rolled off his shoulders. He had no thoughts, no pain, nothing.

"Thadities, are you there?" The words tumbled out of Oak's mouth.

He saw a vision of himself as he centred his body and mind, as he readied himself for sword practice. He moved to an ancient rhythm, as old as time. Now this rhythm flowed through Oak's mind and body, as the dragons wove through the storm and took Oak with them.

"Thadities?" Oak held on tightly and with eyes shut, swayed when Thadities banked left and descended to the ground. Oak glanced around and recognized the field from which they had ascended.

"Oak," said Thadities as pity dripped from his voice. "Wait for me here."

Oak slid down and lay on the ground.

Thadities stalked off towards the other dragons and they stood and talked together. They gestured with their talons and looked over at Oak every now and then. Oak just wondered when the nightmare might end. He was a failure and if he disappeared in a puff of smoke, he wouldn't be missed.

He felt a tap on his shoulder, and as he opened his eyes, he saw the clan had formed a circle and gazed at him with questions emanating from their eyes.

"Oak, the flight home has been abandoned because your flight mastery is deplorable," said Chalice. "We need to rest for a short time and then you can demonstrate to Thadities your flight expertise."

"Flight expertise!" Oak screamed. "Are you mad? I have never flown in my life before!"

Thadities and the clan looked at Oak as if they realised they were in trouble. "Are you really a novice, Oak?" asked Thadities.

He nodded and Thadities picked him up in his teeth and placed him on his back. They moved off to one side, and then the lessons began.

Oak mounted and dismounted until his legs turned to jelly. Then he found a way to twist the rope that Thadities had attached to his head piece, around his wrist. After a few hours of frustration, fun and laughter, Thadities told him that he was satisfied with his progress and he would be taught on every flight during the coming quest.

Thadities joined the clan and after supper they settled down for the night. Oak, worn out, placed his blanket near Thadities, and slept.

Chapter

# SIX

"Oak are you awake?" called Thadities.

Reluctantly, Oak got up and looked up at Thadities. Close-up, he looked like a battle-hardened warrior. Fierce. "Food and then we're going home. Be ready."

Mounting Thadities, Oak thought, at least he wouldn't disgrace himself today. After yesterday's lessons, he knew it in his bones.

One by one, the dragons beat their wings into the wind. Thadities and Oak brought up the rear and they aimed for the sun.

The light-headedness that accompanied the displaced air wasn't so bad today, Oak thought, as he looked for a black hole that would take them to the dragons' homeland.

Beat, beat went their wings as the aged but fearless dragons raced through the sky.

He would not disgrace himself in front of them again. He shouted for joy for the sheer pleasure of being alive and a warrior.

Oak noticed that Thadities' wings beat the air once. A few seconds ago there had been two beats. What had happened? Was something wrong? He noticed his breath was uneven, so he calmed himself down, and started to breathe normally again.

Courage Oak, courage, he thought.

Thadities and Oak caught up with Grumpy and Chalice and he realised the problem. They were caught in a web that covered a black hole. As they tried to dislodge themselves from this sticky substance Oak knew this was serious.

The harder they flung their talons about, the tighter the threads pulled. The webbing seemed to have crawled along their skin and left large welts behind. They screamed and shrieked and yelled out, "Help Thadities, help!"

Thadities turned his head, and said, "Oak curl into a ball and hold on tightly. We are going to blast the web."

Thadities manoeuvred his bulk to face the web and aimed. A golden flame shot out over the web and it bounded back and lit up the sky behind them.

Thadities shouted, "Oak there's something wrong here, there must be a type of force field interwoven amongst the threads. My flame is useless against it." The web shimmered in the sunlight; it glinted as if it wanted to lure them to their deaths and then a blanket of darkness descended and shrouded them all.

Thadities and Oak dropped like stones. Oak held on and Thadities showed great flight mastery until he eyed the ground and then he skimmed Oak's castle, and the ancient trees and landed with a bump in an open field.

The other dragons landed safely, and Chalice and Grumpy were with them.

Chalice stumbled over and spoke to Thadities. "What just happened? We were caught, and then that web retracted its threads, shut its force field off and let us drop out of the sky." Thadities replied, "It may have let you go, but that web now covers our only way home. We cannot penetrate the mass." He checked Grumpy's burnt and damaged skin, and added, "It seems that web oozed a substance that can burn our skins." He swung his head towards Oak. "Oak, do you know anything about a force field covering your homeland?"

"No Thadities," replied Oak. "No one flies here, so how would we know?"

"Where are your kinsfolk, Oak?" continued Thadities. "I saw as we flew over the castle that it is empty. Surely it should be swarming with your kinsfolk?"

Oak sighed. "My kinsfolk have vanished just like the clans. That was why I was where I was, when I was, when you found me." He was startled to realise he hadn't told the dragons this before. He remembered telling Chalice he was a knight-in-training. He had said nothing about the other matter.

"How long ago did they vanish?" asked Thadities.

"Just that day. The day I met Chalice and the rest of your clan." Oak explained how he had gone to sleep in a castle brimming with life and woken to silence. "I started to walk to the village to see if there were any villagers there," he added.

"Then this is the same enemy involved in our land and in this one?" asked Thadities.

"Yes," shouted everyone, as they closed ranks.

Thadities nodded at Chalice while he cast a cursory glance over the camp. Oak was thrilled that he was close to the castle, although he was sad to see it still deserted. He would be able to eat a good meal and change his clothes. He had noticed earlier the dragons were plant eaters. They would not starve while on this quest, but he didn't eat grass.

Thadities called their first council meeting to discuss their plight. Oak and the dragons walked towards the middle of the camp where Chalice had marked out an outer and smaller inner circle with her talons.

Thadities called out to Oak, "Stand in the inner circle." Glancing around at the dragons, he said to them, "Arrange yourselves from highest seniority down. These will be your permanent placements."

Oak stood in the centre, and the dragons arranged themselves in their designated positions. Chalice, Grumpy, Daphadilly, Steffen and Waddle stood shoulder to shoulder and Thadities squeezed in beside Chalice and Waddle.

Thadities wore a brooding expression and the clan looked worried. Oak didn't blame them. They were facing an unseen enemy lurking in the background; an enemy who fought from the depths of darkness and deceit.

Thadities said, "There's something odd going on here on Welddpool as well as at home." He looked at Oak. "It's time to talk about your life before the vanishing."

The vanishing, Oak thought. That was an apt description.

Thadities began his questions. "The disk in the night sky. Did it shine the night your kinsfolk vanished?"

Oak rolled his eyes, and said, "Thadities the moon rises every night. The sun goes down, and the moon take its place; it gives its gift of light to the darkness. On some days my kinsfolk worship the moon by special holidays and feasting days. Don't you have a moon?"

Thadities snorted. "We do, but the moon on our homeland shines down shards of brilliant, white light, not like this whimsy sphere. Our moon is part of our homeland, it joins us as the light crosses over into darkness and stays until they next cross."

"It's not our moon then," Oak said.

Nothing more could be discussed this late into the night, so the meeting was abandoned. Thadities went and lay down, Oak shrugged, patted Thadities' wing and slid underneath with his blanket. He had no answers. Beyond the warm darkness under the dragon's wing, he heard the rest of the clan disperse.

Chapter

# SEVEN

The night passed, and, in the morning, Oak found the clan standing around the centre circle once more. They bellowed and gestured to each other in an alien tongue. Oak was ignored, so he walked to the castle to collect food. He had nearly run out and he did not want hunger to be added to his woes. He had not been back in his home since the vanishing. He needed to gather supplies. He needed a quiet space to think.

Oak tiptoed onto the drawbridge and gingerly walked into the bailey. He took a quick detour to the armoury and sleeping chamber, but nothing had changed. He walked on to the main kitchens. There were signs that rats had nibbled the bread, but it still tasted good. Oak rammed the bread into his mouth, spat out the weevils as they wiggled on his tongue, stuffed more bread into his pockets and left the kitchen. So, the castle wasn't entirely deserted. The people and horses were gone, but rats and weevils remained.

More life awaited his discovery. Why were there butterflies in the bailey? Oak stared at them as he stepped onto the cobbles.

The butterflies flitted closer and skimmed the top of his head.

Oak sneezed as one landed on the tip of his nose. The butterfly clung on and stared him in the eye. Before Oak had realised it wanted to be followed, it had flown half way across the bailey.

Oak ran over the cobbles, banged onto the drawbridge and shot onto the grass. He streaked past some tournament tents, which should have been dismantled had anyone been left to do it. He sighted the butterflies in the distance and his heart sank.

He ran to the edge of the forbidden wildwoods and peered into its gloom. He took his courage into his hands and tried to penetrate a thick hedge growing across the edge of the wildwoods. On closer inspection he saw the hedge was made from woven tree limbs that rested one upon another until it reached an alarming height. The tree limbs were alive.

Oak's kinsfolk had never attempted to forage or hunt in the forbidden wildwoods. An evil air emanated from it, as if the wildwoods itself kept everybody out. It was known around the district that many had entered over the years, never to be seen again. Mothers scolded their children with the threat that they would disappear into its depths if they didn't behave themselves.

He looked for his sword hilt and found it gone. His heart jolted, and he thought, it must have slipped through my belt.

He threw his shoulders back, placed one foot onto the bottom tree limb and started to scale the woven hedge. He skimmed each row and then balanced his fingertips onto the top limb. A beam of sunlight hit his shoulder blades and bounced into the gloom beyond, and this miracle gave Oak time to place his foot on the other side. Before Oak had gained a foothold, a plaited vine wound around his right foot, pulled him towards the ground and flung him forwards until he found himself on a foul pathway. He patted himself down and found he had no injuries, so he stood up and walked cautiously forward. Towering mounds of unknown matter were dotted about, and they loomed at him as he brushed past. In one place, this putrid mess had toppled across the pathway and blocked any further movement from Oak. He glared at the butterflies just up ahead.

The ground shook, the tree limbs shifted and hemmed him in. Oak recognised the oak, ash and beech, some with massive ancient trunks, others no more than young saplings. He looked at the undergrowth and knew there is no help there; it was impenetrable. The pathway was the only way in and out.

Oak shouted, "What is this? Am I being held for ransom?"

A dreadful moan poured through the wildwoods. Was it a cry of distressed consciousness? Sap ran down the outside of the trees' bark, formed a sticky river and drippled onto the pathway.

Oak was more puzzled than frightened, and he decided to battle his way through the putrid mess and confront the butterflies which had led him here. He tried to move forward, and a tree branch slapped him in the face.

"Ouch!" he called out involuntarily. 'That hurt.' A small amount of blood dripped onto his vest. 'What's the matter with you?" he yelled, as he rubbed his cheek.

The butterflies re-joined the largest oak tree and they continued to taunt Oak. What had he done? Nothing. He had never entered the forbidden wildwoods before today. He had never felled a tree. He had never killed a butterfly and never, ever, had he impaled and displayed them on the castle walls as some of his kinsfolk had done.

There was a clue to the mystery here, he felt it in his bones. Thadities must be told.

Oak called out to the butterflies. "Excuse me, would you guide me to the edge of the wildwoods, please? I don't trust the pathway because it winds its way around the trees and even if I could get moving at all, it might lead me who knows where."

The ground shifted, tree roots moved, and one butterfly joined him. Oak sighed. This was madness; how was he going to be believed?

The butterfly flitted ahead of him and Oak started to run after it, thankful the trees let him through. As he traced his footsteps back to the field, an awful aroma settled in his nostrils. The trees stank, and Oak called out, "The trees smell all wrong. Why is that?"

There was no reply.

He dallied no longer, but ran back towards the woven hedge. He placed his foot on its first bough and Oak wondered if it was assisting him instead of hindering him to reach its other side. He didn't stop until he had left the forbidden woods behind him.

He looked back and saw that the single butterfly had stayed at the edge of the wildwoods. It watched over him until he had cleared the field.

He ran so fast he had a stich in his side by the time he reached camp, and he gasped as he called, "Thadities, there are butterflies over yonder! They bewitched me! I followed them to the forbidden wildwoods. When I started to climb the woven hedge, it pulled me in and flung me onto a putrid pathway, and—"

"Oak, slow down," boomed Thadities.

"Sorry." He caught his breath and started again. He told Thadities he had followed some butterflies into the forbidden wildwoods, was held hostage by some nasty trees, and now the butterflies waited at the edge of the wildwoods for him to return. Was this the sign they needed to solve the vanishing?

"Are you mad, Oak?" asked Thadities. "You followed butterflies into an unknown wildwoods and then became a hostage!" He called the clan together.

"At least I found out something," grumbled Oak.

Thadities snorted, but he and the others followed Oak to the wildwoods.

Thadities pushed against the hedge, and the hedge pushed back. Every time the dragons forced their bulk onto its woven limbs, they were repelled. Thadities turned and said to Oak, "The hedge should have damaged limbs somewhere by now. I'll find them." He strolled off as if he didn't have a care in the world. Oak was impressed by his nonchalance.

Oak kept a wary eye on the hedge as Thadities stopped, every now and then, and peered into its gloomy depths. Suddenly, Thadities was knocked off his talons and thrown onto his back.

Oak ran, and waves of energy erupted from the wildwoods, and knocked him to the ground. Winded, he looked around and watched as Thadities scrambled up and helped most of the older dragons back onto their talons. They had also been knocked over, but they seemed unhurt.

Thadities called out, "Take care! These trees emit energy waves identical to the ones from the web."

Unhurt, they regrouped and returned to camp. Thadities shooed the clan towards the circle and Chalice spoke up. "Oak and Thadities will fly reconnaissance over the canopies, then any skulduggery behaviour can be reported to the clan."

Oak's heart beat a fast tattoo as he climbed onto Thadities' back. He thumped his bottom onto the indentation and wrapped the hanging cord tightly around his palm and wrist, glanced over at Chalice and hung on. Only a short time ago this routine terrified him; now he brimmed over with pride that he had mastered the climb.

Thadities took off and as they glided over the castle walls Oak glanced into the bailey; empty. They arrived on the west side of the wildwoods and searched for cover from the canopies of the tallest trees. Thadities' wings dipped and dived into the leaves, but he was unable to find the butterflies.

The wildwood was an impenetrable pool of darkness. Thadities crossed the trees in a zig zag manoeuvre and millions of leaves rippled in his wake, but Oak saw nothing of the butterflies. They re-crossed twice more, and then a fearsome mask enveloped the tree canopies and it smiled.

Thadities gave their pre-arranged signal to let Oak know they were going back to camp.

On arriving back at camp Thadities and Oak reported to the elders. The elders took a vote to revisit old strategies, especially the ones they had used as young warriors. They would try to find any parallels or anything at all that would help with the quest.

Oak walked to the castle. He needed to collect more food and to visit the armoury. He needed to check the armour and weapons for any signs of deterioration, as without a blacksmith on site, they could never be repaired or replaced.

Oak looked over the armour and weapons and was pleased all was in order. He picked up a new sword, as he had been unable to find his lost one, ran his thumb down the sharp blade and liked the way it felt in his hand. He then tucked the steel securely into his belt.

He entered the kitchen, collected bread, fruit and fermented ale, found a comfortable spot, sat down and let his thoughts roam.

The butterflies had enticed him away from the castle. He had followed them willy-nilly with no thoughts of any danger and had entered the forbidden wildwoods. That was mad. No, not mad; insane.

"Oak," shouted Daffadilly, as she poked her head over the castle wall. The sun reflected off her eyewear glass and she squinted before she said, "Thadities sent me to find you. You must come back to camp."

He was blinded by a sharp pain as it shot through his skull, and as he walked beside Daffadilly at a snail's pace, she adjusted her stride to accommodate his. Was this friendship?

They arrived together, and he noticed that Thadities stood on the outer circle. They both hurried and joined the clan. Oak sat in the centre and said, "Sorry Thadities, elders, I have a blinding headache. I have suffered from them since I was a page, and I ask for your forgiveness for my bad manners."

Waddle placed a hearing trumpet against her ear and as she shuffled forward she said, "Oak, we have a potion for headaches. It is made from a herb called feverfew." She left the circle and returned with a brown liquid in a vial. Oak swallowed the potion, Waddle patted his head and she re-joined the circle.

Within a short time Oak's head started to feel better and as he glanced up at Waddle, she caught his eye and nodded.

Thadities said, "Warriors, we have been shepherded by a master manipulator. Oak sighted butterflies because he was meant to sight them. It was not a random assignation, so it has to be connected to the vanished. The trees are intelligent, and they enticed Oak with a bold game of the leader must be followed. If the trees had wanted Oak and we dragons assassinated, they would have acted to have us killed. The purpose of our being lured to Oak's homeland must soon be revealed. The trees and plants are not the antagonists; they just tried to get our attention, in the most extraordinary of ways."

The clan looked bewildered.

Thadities asked Oak to explain how he knew the trees were distressed.

Oak sighed and said, "I just knew the trees were distressed. These unwanted thoughts ran through my head while I was at the castle."

"Is it something to do with you, Oak? With who you are?" Thadities prompted.

Oak sighed again. "I have no idea. I don't know who I am, exactly."

"How can that be?" Chalice prompted.

"I don't know my sire's name. I am no descendant of royalty because Sir Glyneath knows things like that, and he would have boasted about it if I had been. I don't know why I was placed in one of my homeland's largest castles. I was never told. I have no idea of my lineage, but I have been kicked around enough times to know I am probably a bastard."

He looked around to see what the dragons thought, but it was difficult to tell.

"My heritage became less important to me when I became tied to Sir Glyneath. The life of a squire is hard work, and thoughts of my sire and mother diminished over the years. If they sneak in unannounced, I tell them to 'begone'."

Thadities turned to Oak and asked, "Are the trees connected to you in any way?"

"No, Thadities," replied Oak. "They cried out in a low murmured whisper and I felt how desolate they were. I felt it down to my bones, but a connection, no."

Thadities and the clan walked through the field and stepped gingerly around the wild flowers that had sprung up everywhere since they visited the wildwoods.

"Where have they spouted from?" asked Oak but the dragons had no answers.

Too soon they arrived at the fringe of the wildwoods.

Silence bounded out to greet them and was closely followed by a malevolent air.

Oak started to breathe erratically and Thadities loped over and asked, "What's the matter, Oak?"

Oak pointed towards the wildwoods as the air shimmered up and down the tree trunks.

Oak thought Thadities approached the barrier with some trepidation, while he moved towards the trees with a light, but apprehensive heart. They climbed up the barrier side by side, just in case Thadities fell backwards and squashed him in a fall. When they reached the top, to Oak's amazement, it held. Thadities wobbled back and forth for a bit, and then he dug his talons into the wood. He grabbed Oak's hair with a talon and then they were both flung through the air, arms, legs and talons flailing, until they landed on their backsides on the crazed pathway.

Oak smelt again an underhanded, thick and shadowy malevolence in the air. It also snaked deep into the centre of his bone marrow. He turned to Thadities, and said, "Are you troubled?"

"No, Oak. Are you feeling uneasy about entering the woods? Try not to worry," replied Thadities.

Oak noticed it had darkened, and the trees had intertwined their canopies and blocked the sun so effectively, not a shard of light showed. Their limbs had woven into their neighbours' and the wildwoods' floor looked depressed and forlorn. Oak looked up at Thadities and then they both looked to the sky for answers.

Oak leaned on Thadities, and as he kept one eye on the tree canopies, he checked for his sword hilt. It was not there. He had lost another sword.

Silently the butterflies returned and were now garlanded throughout the ancient oak tree.

"Thadities!" Oak called.

The butterflies just stared right through him.

Oak and Thadities stood in front of the aged tree and Oak asked, "Do you have a common language? Why have we been brought before the ancient trees? What does the wildwoods want from us?"

The forest leapt into life, and the trees beat their branches against one another's trunks, and banged the ground before them, and howled.

Oak was rooted to the ground, and as he placed one foot before the other, he brushed up against Thadities and started to climb upwards. The air shimmered and shook and grabbed Oak's vest, but he clung on to Thadities and finally he burrowed into his neck. Thadities threw his wing into an updraft and then in a heartbeat they were dragged sideways, into a whirling vortex. Oak was beyond thought as the wind shook him until his teeth rattled and then it tried to shred his skin from his bones.

A vice wrapped itself around his skull and he screamed, 'Thadities," but it was only a whimper as he clung onto Thadities with terrified fingers.

Within the next heartbeat they were pulled into a spiral of silence; they had entered the centre of the whirling circle of madness. Around and around they were flung, and as debris latched on to his body, his brain stopped working and he prayed to every saint in heaven. It was no saint that heard him, but Thadities.

Thadities had moved underneath him. He opened his mouth and out spewed a red and gold flame. It wound its way up the spiral and shot over the lip of the vortex and Oak prayed the clan had stayed below and watched for any odd signs. . .

Oak ducked his head as a large piece of tree trunk whizzed by, and it lodged itself into Thadities' wing.

"Damn," Oak cursed. "Hold on, Thadities."

Blood poured from the wound, and Thadities' wing drooped into the whirling air. The vortex just kept up its hideous momentum, while the debris danced to its own master's voice and Oak wondered how it would end.

He nearly reached the wound, but the velocity of the wind pushed him back into Thadities' neck.

"Thadities we're not being spun around so fast now," he shouted. "I'm not so giddy, how about you?"

Oak looked skywards for some saintly guidance and saw the sky had turned a wrinkly green as the old dragons crowded in.

Tears rolled down Oak's face, and he gave thanks to that perfect wrinkly green colour. Thadities had grown weaker and Oak had thought if they were not found soon they would both be likened to stones that had sunk to the bottom of the vortex. Now they were to be rescued.

The dragons' beautiful faces peered down, while horror shone from their eyes. Their eyewear had never looked so fine, Oak thought.

He saw their heads arranged in a rough circle around the vortex rim. Chalice dipped down and grabbed Thadities by the scuff of his neck, and she held him gently in her teeth. Oak held on for dear life and they were both wrenched out of the cylinder.

Oak saw that each member of the clan had gripped the one in front, and while they waited, they stayed attached.

Oak opened his mouth and croaked. His lungs hurt.

"Shush Oak," said Chalice as she checked him and Thadities over.

Blood seeped from Thadities' wound and had trickled down into the vortex.

Thadities was placed onto Grumpy's back and Chalice instructed Steffen to hold one of his wings while she took the other. Oak was transferred to Waddle's back; a first for them both.

Chapter

# EIGHT

The flight was slow and dangerous, but Chalice was a smart leader and they all glided into camp safely. Steffen and Chalice rolled Thadities onto his back, checked his wound and waited for Waddle.

Oak dismounted, thanked Waddle and went and stood next to Thadities.

"We need clean water, cloths, and herbs, Oak," she called. "I will fetch them, but will you wait for my return?"

Chalice looked relived but annoyed and replied, "Waddle knows how to dress wounds and Thadities' wound isn't deep. You must not be worried." She looked at him closely and said, "Are you hurt?"

"No, I was bumped about but not hurt," Oak replied. "Are you annoyed?"

"Yes, Oak, I am very angry. I've called a council meeting," Chalice replied, as she propelled them both forward.

Apart from Waddle, the clan was arranged around the circle. Oak stood in its centre, tall and proud. Chalice glared, and the dragons looked behind and saw they were not aligned. Their tails, hearing aids, necks and heads were not shoulder to shoulder, so they shuffled around until they stood talon to talon. Steffen must have realized his bum was still a bit out, for he shuffled forward a little. Perfect.

"Dragon warriors must be disciplined," Chalice barked. "Today, because you've not followed any protocol, we nearly lost Thadities and Oak. Luckily, Thadities is not seriously hurt, and will be able to fly when he has healed. Oak has not suffered any injuries. Oak and Thadities went off, willy-nilly without any thought of the consequences, and brought disaster down on to their heads. Their foolishness nearly led to their deaths, and the end of the quest before it has even begun."

Chalice continued, "From now on, your belongings must be kept tidy; your armour and weapons are your responsibility. Thadities and I will not tolerate any disobedience from those who serve us. Turn to the dragon next to you and remember their face. At every moment, you must know where this dragon is. Not knowing might get them killed. Does everybody understand these commands?"

"Yes, we understand," a loud chorus of voices shouted.

Chalice peered down at Oak and said, "Thadities and Oak will look out for each other. Understood?"

"Yes, Chalice, I understand. Sorry," replied Oak.

He looked over at the clan and saw a different set to their shoulders. Before him stood brave warriors, not aged, retired dragons. Oak was proud to have been invited to be part of this strong and vigorous dragon clan.

Chalice gave Oak permission to pay a visit to the castle and said, "You must collect food, water and more blankets for Thadities. It has got cooler in the night and he must be kept warm."

Oak was relieved. He left the camp without a thought in his head except that his sword needed to be replaced. He entered the armoury, found a wicked sword with a sharp blade, tucked it into his belt and ran to the kitchens. The big doors stood ajar, and he streaked straight into a wooden table, which brought him up abruptly. "Ouch!" he yelled.

He wasn't hungry but decided to collect some apples from the underground storage room. It would help increase his meagre food store. As he descended the stairs the cold invaded his bones.

He entered the first of the storerooms and cursed the saints that he had not helped with the harvest last year. Oak scratched his head in perplexity, and wondered which boxes contained the freshest apples. Then, out of the corner of his eye, he caught sight of a shadow as it drifted down the hallway.

They'd all been told by Chalice they must report to the clan when they needed to be helped. Was this such a time?

"Nah," he muttered, and followed the shadow. "Ouch," he yelped, as his back scraped against a hook, buried deep into the stone wall. He knew he needed to be invisible and yelping gave the shadow his position.

You idiot, Oak thought.

Oak kept a little more air between them and started to tiptoe forward. Water dripped down the castle's slimy walls and ran into channels embedded into the stone floor. He stumbled over something that moved. He hoped it was only rats. He found himself on a dark staircase that led on to an even darker corridor. He felt relieved. He knew this place; it was used for extra storage when there had been a bumper harvest. Oak wondered if he should have waited until the dragons were outside in the courtyard before he began this stupid shadow chase. Chalice would have insisted he carry his sword and a lighted torch. Well, he had the sword.

He gathered his tattered nerves and descended the steps. Towards the end of the staircase the corridor turned right. As quiet as a mouse, Oak tiptoed towards the door, placed his hand on the edge of the wood and shoved it open. He eyes slewed around the gloomy room, but he saw only the ghostly outlines of boxes and barrels that were stowed on the cold hard floor.

"Stand up with your hands pointed towards the ceiling," Oak shouted into the darkness.

The silence hurt Oak's ears and his heart. Was nobody here? He had hoped there was someone.

Scrape, scrape. Oak looked over and watched a barrel move. A knight stood up and strode over to Oak. His walk was funny. His stride was small, and he swayed from side to side, in a most peculiar way. The knight sidled up to Oak, lifted his arms and removed his helmet.

Oak looked into the startled face of a young girl. She seemed not much older than him.

"Who. . . who are you?" cried Oak.

"I am Forthwind," the girl replied, as she placed her helmet on the storeroom floor. She then threaded her fingers into her long, dark curly hair and started to shake out the mass. She stopped abruptly and looked him over and asked, "Who are you and what are you doing in this castle?"

"Forthwind, come back upstairs to the kitchen and we'll talk," said Oak. "Are you hungry?"

Forthwind bent down, picked up her helmet and followed Oak back to the castle's kitchens. He offered Forthwind a chair, moved over to the ovens, raked together some old embers and re-ignited the fire. Oak rummaged through the shelves in the cold larder for food that didn't have weevils and mould throughout it, and as he glanced outside he saw two dragon's necks draped over the castle walls.

Oak rushed outside and found Grumpy and Chalice fascinated by a palfrey. The horse had waited patiently at the kitchen door for Forthwind to return, and as Oak moved closer to the dragons he said, "Wait here."

He returned to the kitchen and said, "Come out into the courtyard. My clan has decided to decorate the castle walls with their faces and your explanations can wait."

Forthwind gave Oak her hand and he steered her into the courtyard. Oak held onto her hand very tightly in case she decided to bolt. He soon found Forthwind was made of sterner stuff than that. She looked up into the dragons' excited faces and curtsied to them both.

She was not quite as tall as Oak but her features and hair looked remarkably like his. Both the dragons bowed back and extended their talons as Forthwind walked tall and unafraid towards them.

"Welcome, little one, our wait is over. The clan is completed," Chalice said, as tears dribbled from her eyes.

Oak was shocked. What... what was happening here. Was this slip of a girl the other great knight?

Chalice glared at Oak as if she'd heard his childish words, and he blushed to the roots of his hair in embarrassment. After all their kindness and the friendship he had been shown, this is how he felt; envious of a girl he had just met!

Oak returned to the kitchens and collected the food from the larder. They sat down on the cobbles, with their backs up against a stone wall and Oak said, "Forthwind, eat your food. When we leave the castle and return to camp, there will be very little food there. You and I will often come back to the castle to collect food, clothes, blankets, armour and weapons."

Forthwind ate obediently while Chalice retold her tale.

"On returning to our homeland we found all of our kinsfolk had disappeared in the same way as your kinsfolk have disappeared from your homeland. Thadities went to see our seer Owl and found his cave empty but the ancient book with the old notes scribbled in the margins was open on his table. Thadities read the tale and realised we must seek two legendary knights on a homeland called Welddpool. We found you, Oak, but not the other. Now we've found Forthwind the legend is fulfilled."

"Who are you, Forthwind?" called out Chalice. "The clan met Oak some time ago, but you've not appeared until now."

"Don't be alarmed by Chalice's question, Forthwind," said Oak, trying to make up for his earlier envy. "Just tell us how you came to be in the castle. I and the clan have searched the castle many times before today, and it has always been empty."

Forthwind stood up and nearly overbalanced on her armour-clad legs. "I don't know where I was or how I arrived," she told Chalice. "My first coherent thought was, where am I? Why was I dressed in armour? I'm a maid-in-waiting and have been since I was a child. This Castle is a mystery to me. My mistress is Lord Darkley's lady and they live at Snowdon Castle."

Oak believed her. Chalice and Grumpy looked as if they did too. Oak had never heard of Castle Snowdon, but one thing he believed. Forthwind would not choose to wear armour; it was too heavy for a girl.

Forthwind said to Oak, "I need to change out of this armour."

Oak showed her to his lady's chamber, and she found piles of discarded clothing on a large chair. She turned her back and dressed. She dressed quickly for a girl, Oak thought, and when she turned around she wore a beautiful bejewelled gown, the hem of which just skimmed the floor as she walked.

Oak and Forthwind soon joined the dragons in the bailey. Chalice bent her neck over the wall and Oak took Forthwind's hand and helped her climb her first dragon. She was undaunted. When they reached the indent, they both sat, and Oak said to her, "Forthwind, wind the rope around your hand and hold on."

Excitement poured out of her eyes and she took the rope Oak held out to her, wound it around her hand and smiled.

Oak was aware that danger lurked in the atmosphere and had sunk deep into his bones, but were Chalice and Grumpy aware there was a story still to be told?

Chalice was lead dragon. She beat the air and hurtled into a head wind. They were off.

They arrived back at camp, and Forthwind and Oak slid from Chalice's back and walked towards Thadities, who looked better but who was quiet.

"Thadities," Oak called softly.

Thadities propped himself up and peered at Forthwind and Oak. "Are they related?" he asked.

"No," they both said simultaneously.

Oak said, "Thadities, you know I don't know who my parents were."

Forthwind said, "I don't know either. I've been bound into service forever."

Thadities snorted and said, "This mystery is unfathomable."

The dragons draw closer to Thadities and waited to be introduced.

"Forthwind, these are Oak's clan," Chalice said. "You know Grumpy and me. This is Thadities and these are Daphadilly, Steffen and Waddle. Go with Oak and Waddle now, and they'll show you where we all sleep. You could bed down near Oak and Thadities if you're scared."

The next morning Oak and Forthwind rose late. The camp was in disarray and the dragons had vanished.

Oak tore across the camp and shouted, "Thadities!" He threw himself upon the dragon and called out, "Where are the clan, Thadities?"

"Silence," he barked as he held out a talon. "Steffen was missed this morning. A search party was put together, and they have gone as far as the edge of the wildwoods."

Not long after that, the clan clattered back into camp, minus Steffen.

Waddle said, "We searched around the edge of the wildwoods and there was no sight of him."

They all knew that Steffen was a stickler for rules; he would not have left the camp without a strong reason.

Thadities called for volunteers. The wildwoods needed to be scoured from the air.

Daffadilly's and Waddle's talons shot up into the air. Waddle peered over her eyewear, glanced at Daffadilly, and said, "We're not ancient fuddy-duddies; we are retired warriors and we demand flight time."

They got the nod. They removed their shawls and flung them to the ground. Daffadilly's hearing trumpet soon followed, and then, while Waddle fiddled with the wire of her eyewear, they walked together towards the clearing. They dipped their wings into a slight head wind and soared into the sky, turned towards the wildwoods and were lost from sight.

Oak and Forthwind turned and listened to Thadities and Chalice. Thadities said, "Should they have gone without a grown up to supervise them?"

"Thadities, they might be old, but they are not senile. You need all your kinsfolk to be prepared for battle and Oak has told me that Pembrokeshire Castle is stuffed with many weapons. So far, there are two children, me and four elderly dragons; we all must be trained. Immediately," said Chalice, as she frowned. "Thadities you are a highly decorated warrior, and now you must train all of us to become a cohesive clan, one you'll be proud of."

Before Thadities replied, the sky darkened as three dragons glided down into the clearing. Steffen hit the ground first, rushed over and said, "I'm sorry. I didn't expect to have been so long. I went for a short walk and spied some stones in the distance that looked as if they'd sprouted out of the ground. I inspected the stones and realised they were ancient standing stones that hadn't been there last night. The marks were from an ancient bardic alphabet used to form a secret language called Ogham. It was a secret language and is somehow connected to the trees," said Steffen. "I studied this ancient language when I was in my second year of coding. It still turns up occasionally, especially on homelands that had an elemental lineage."

They all looked stunned and Oak and Forthwind joined hands and ran around in a circle. They laughed and shouted, "Steffen is a clever clog, Steffen is a clever clog."

Thadities called a council meeting. He rose from his bed and stood on the outer circle. Oak took Forthwind's hand again and guided her to the centre circle.

Thadities asked, "Are there any scribes amongst us?

Oak, Forthwind and Steffen moved. Oak knew about Steffen, he was the dragons' code breaker extraordinaire, but Forthwind; a lady's maid?

Forthwind said, "I was taught to read and write and was one of the castle scribes. Now, I look after my lady's affairs."

Thadities continued, "Daffadilly and Waddle flew a successful mission today. Well done."

Daffadilly's skin turned a darker shade of green. Oak realised that Daffadilly was embarrassed. He knew all about treacherous skin and the awful way it changed colour.

"Ow," Oak yelled, as a frisson went up and down his spine.

The clan peered down and Thadities asked, "What happened?"

"I felt a sharp pain run up and down my spine. It's gone now," Oak replied.

The dragons moved away from the circle and Oak said to Thadities, "We need your permission to go to the castle and collect food."

"Yes of course; and would you take Daffadilly? She was our armoury master and from today she will be reinstated in that post as well as being your new tutor. We need to know what the armoury holds."

Oak and Forthwind spied Daffadilly in the distance and went to join her. They both congratulated her on her new position and as she smiled down upon them she sighed and replied, "Thank you, Oak and Forthwind. Now, we'll be off. I have not visited any armoury for far too long."

After they arrived at the castle drawbridge, Oak and Forthwind entered the bailey and walked toward the silent armoury, both knowing their assigned tasks. Daffadilly stood outside and draped her neck over the castle wall, adjusted her eye wear and waited for the armour to be brought into the bailey.

Oak opened the door, peered into the gloom and noticed all was in order; nothing had been touched. Dust lay about, but he decided to say nothing about it. He doesn't want to dust today. He recalled a talk he had with Thadities about polished armour, when he was told that armour that shone let your enemies know where you were hidden. He knew that dust and unpolished armour were not the same, so he kept his mouth shut.

Daffadilly asked Forthwind, "What did you do with your armour?"

"Upstairs in the lady's chamber," she replied. She ran off and collected the armour. She returned and dropped the precious armour onto the bailey's floor, where it banged and clanked as it bounced among the cobbles.

"Hey," objected Oak. "Our armour and weapons are precious, they can't be repaired or replaced because the blacksmiths have vanished. All equipage must be honoured and cherished."

Forthwind looked annoyed and she flicked her hair as she passed Oak. Every now and then Oak heard her bang down a piece of metal and he hoped she felt better.

Oak and Forthwind were very tired at the end of the inspection but Daffadilly was pleased with the amassment of weapons, armour and tools that had been found in the armoury. Inside an old cupboard, tucked up at the back of the room was a stack of clothes. Forthwind changed immediately. She stepped out into the bailey and Daffadilly and Oak both stared.

She was dressed in leggings, boots, undershirt and vest; over these she'd slung a longbow, complete with nasty looking arrows.

"Are you a good shot?" shouted Oak.

"I'm an excellent shot. I've practised for years, without anybody's knowledge. The longbow is an extension of my arm," replied Forthwind.

Oak dressed then, and collected shin-guards, thigh-plates, chainmail shirts, knee-joints, helmets, nasal and neck-flaps; everything he needed for the days ahead. He went and stood in front of Daffadilly, who smiled.

They looked through the weapons and found lances, more longbows and arrows, broadswords, and some longswords. There were no great swords but both Forthwind and Oak were too small to wield these great swords anyway. They choose swords they could wield against an enemy. They didn't choose daggers, spears or other assorted weapons because they had no knowledge of how to use them to their advantage.

Daffadilly, Oak and Forthwind left the castle with assorted weapons tucked under their wings and arms and headed back to camp.

"Forthwind," said Daffadilly. "the armour you wore on the day you were found. Who did it belong to?"

Oak listened and waited for her explanation. He hadn't spoken to Forthwind about her sudden appearance without Thadities' permission, for they had a rule; no quest or clan folk were to be questioned like a common thief.

Forthwind thought for a moment and proceeded to tell her story. "I don't know. I remember I dressed my lady for supper and then I found myself in this castle's kitchens in full armour."

"Well!" chortled Daffadilly. "How could you have been plucked from one castle and then left at another? Have we been told the truth?"

Oak looked up at Daffadilly, and said, "You encountered me in an odd place."

"Of course, Oak," Daffadilly replied. "We all found one another in the oddest places."

A council meeting was called. Oak and Forthwind walked to the middle of the circle and waited for the dragons to arrange themselves around the outer rim. Oak was getting used to these summonses and waited for the next set of commands from Thadities. He hoped it was a flight mission.

The dragons stooped and looked them over. Oak stood so tall he knew if he held up his hand, he could touch the sky. He noticed Forthwind stood on the tips of her toes and he smiled to himself.

Oak listened to Thadities as he spoke quietly. "It's time for Oak and Forthwind to practise with the quintain. Daffadilly has checked, and all is ready and they don't need an audience, understand?"

"Forthwind," called Oak as they entered the field, "I won the quintain tournament on the King's feasting day."

Forthwind shouted, "I need to be shown how to duck my head when the arm swings around."

He took a lance, ran forward and threw, hard. It connected with the heart of the shield and quivered. He returned to Forthwind.

He stood behind her, placed the lance in her hand and explained how to hold and throw a lance. Within minutes, she placed an oversized lance in her delicate hand and ran towards the shield. She looked back at Oak and aimed for the heart of the shield. The lance slammed into its heart, she ducked her head under the quintain arm, ran back and stood next to him, as puzzlement shone from her face.

"Oh, Oak," she yelled. "What happened?"

"How were you able to hit its heart?" he shouted.

Daffadilly had watched from the sidelines and she now shuffled over and joined the chatter. "Right you two, I watched you practise, but it was only one run. It could have been a fluke. You need to practise for a little longer.

"Yes, Daffadilly," cried Oak. "One question; has the quintain been lowered? The last time I competed in a tournament, I was astride my horse and the quintain was higher. We could have used Forthwind's horse, but it has disappeared from the bailey."

"Yes," Daffadilly replied to both questions.

Forthwind picked up her lance and ran towards the shield. Oak watched and noticed her hesitation just before she threw. She hit the centre of the shield, ducked her head under the arm, and ran back once again.

Oak picked up his lance and ran towards the shield. He hit the centre, ducked his head under the arm, and ran back with a frown.

"Daffadilly," Oak said, as he rolled his eyes, "there's something very wrong here."

He looked over at Forthwind, and said, "She was a lady's maid not a knight-in-training." He turned back to the girl. "Why did you hesitate for a second just before you threw the lance?"

"Did I?" she replied. "I have no idea why."

Daffadilly, Oak and Forthwind collected their weapons and returned to camp, puzzled.

Thadities glided down onto his designated spot and started to shout as he hit the ground, "Chalice, in a day or two, I want the children made ready for flight practice. We'll gauge the weather each morning and be guided by the winds."

A surprised air hung about the other dragons. Oak said, "I gave Thadities an oath of fealty; do you require one from Forthwind?"

"No," said Thadities in a surprised voice. "I am your liege lord and I require no further alliances, and Forthwind is not required to ally herself to the dragons. The dragons will now decide, amongst themselves, who will become her guide and mentor."

Grumpy stepped forward and looked at Forthwind and she looked back at him. A bond of sorts had been formed.

That evening around the fire, Thadities said, "Oak's homeland has followed its natural rhythm for centuries. The sun rose and set, and the crossings of the seasons arrived on time. Why were they not warned by the trees that the vanishing was just on their horizon?" Thadities shifted his considerable bulk and continued, "Oak had no knowledge of the web, but the trees seem to a have a knowledge of him. Today, Steffen recognised markings on some standing stones. He has told me the marks run from bottom to top and this is how it is to be read. Steffen believes it's an ancient tree language. Tomorrow, Oak, Forthwind and Steffen will be at the library; they won't return until they have searched every book for those ancient markings."

Steffen nodded his head in agreement.

Chapter

# NINE

The next morning, the three of them set off for the castle's library, and Oak noticed the grass was white and stiff. Frost. Their boots crunched as they crossed the field and Oak stretched his cloak tightly across his shoulders. The seasons had nearly crossed over and the quest had not even begun. Thadities must be told.

Steffen's talons were frozen by the time they reached the drawbridge. He streamed a flame of fire across the tops of his nails to thaw them.

"That feels better," he told Oak and Forthwind.

They entered the bailey, and Oak shot off and collected warmer cloaks. Oak and Forthwind placed theirs around their shoulders but Steffen declined. Steffen waited at the castle walls and Oak and Forthwind went to the library and started to collect the books.

Each book that was brought from the library was placed on Steffen's right. When Steffen had read through the pages and found no symbols written there, it was placed onto his left. If there was anything of importance found, that book was to be placed in front.

The bailey was covered in shadows by the time the shelves were empty. The pile on the left was full of tottering books, the pile in front was empty and the library shelves were bare.

Oak returned to the room for one last look. He placed the ladder against the shelves and ran his hand over each surface, making sure all the dark corners were checked. His hand bumped up against something, something soft. Pulling himself up onto the top rung, he spied a small book, his heart started to pound when he saw symbols on its spine, he grabbed the book and slid down the ladder.

"Steffen, Steffen," he cried, as he waved the book in the air. "There is one more, we missed it because it lived in a dark and forgotten corner."

Steffen looked at the symbols on its spine and first page and made a funny sound in his throat.

They had found the book of symbols and their meanings.

Steffen returned to camp and Oak and Forthwind replaced the books, any which way, so they could be back at camp before darkness fell.

When they arrived, Oak ran up to Thadities and said, "Thadities, the seasons are crossing over and there was a white frost this morning that covered the grass. Do you have crossing over seasons on your homeland?"

"Yes," said Thadities. "There is an urgency now to the quest. Winter and dragons are not well-matched. I am well pleased, Oak, with you and Forthwind, for finding the book of symbols. Steffen has asked for parchment, quill and ink; are these things to be found at the castle?"

"Yes, Thadities," replied Oak. "I will fetch them in the morning."

Oak had collected the last of the mouldy bread without too many weevils, fruit and the last of the salted meat before he left the castle. These he shared with Forthwind while they pondered on their good fortune on finding the book of symbols, and what that meant for them all.

"Are the dragons meat eaters?" asked Forthwind.

"No," replied Oak. "They are plant eaters with heaps of fresh food around for them to munch on."

They turned in for the night, and Oak was up early and, on his way, to collect the writing things for Steffen before the sun had risen. He had wondered in the night if his mastery as a scribe might be of assistance to Steffen this morning.

Taking the steps two at a time he entered his Lord's study, and soon found the writing things strewn over his desk, covered in a thick layer of dust, but otherwise fine.

With a spring in his step he left the castle behind, and ran towards camp. On his return he found Steffen and Northwind waiting for him.

"Oh, good lad, you have brought the writing things," said Steffen.

The three of them made themselves comfortable on some fallen logs and started to unravel the symbols. Oak was asked to be scribe, and he copied the symbols diligently from the standing stone onto the parchment, and as he scratched the lines he thought he had no idea what these markings might mean.

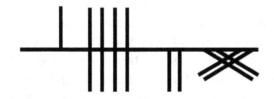

Steffen then asked that he write the letters under each symbol, so that he was able to make sense of their placement.

# HELP

Each letter then formed a word that was placed in order to form the message. It was like putting a puzzle together, Oak thought.

When the message showed itself, Steffen went and fetched Thadities.

Thadities held the parchment in his talons and said to the clan, "This message is a cry for help from the wildwoods. I, Oak and Forthwind will enter the wildwoods tomorrow and we will be ready for any unimaginable crises that might arise."

Muttering was heard coming from the clan, but one quelling look from Thadities and they were quiet.

The clan talked well into the darkness and slept where they lay. Most were asleep within a short time, but Oak was too keyed up to even rest his eyes.

After a restless night, the three of them walked towards the wildwoods with trepidation, while Thadities held the parchment aloft in his talon, like a white flag of surrender.

When they reached the hedge, it unravelled its limbs and allowed them to enter the forbidden wildwoods. No crazed trees stood guard this morning, no whispering leaves followed their footfalls, no nasty smells wafted up their noses. Oak slewed his eyes from side to side looking for any signs of derangement coming from deep within the wildwoods.

They were shown into a clearing, and Oak saw an ancient oak tree that was half tree and half what? he thought. He blinked, looked away, but no, it was true, the ancient oak that stood in front of him was half tree and half elemental.

Oak took a quick glance at Thadities and Forthwind, but there they stood, solid, with looks of amazement spread over their faces.

With his long limbs, the ancient tree gestured them forward, while thousands of leaves turned and watched as they were welcomed to the wildwoods.

Thadities told the ancient oak they had been able to decode the message and that was why they had entered the forbidden wildwoods. He held out the parchment and the oak tree took a cursory glance. Thadities was always thorough, Oak thought.

The ancient oak bade them welcome in a tongue they all understood.

"My name is Fielding," he said. "What are yours?"

"I am Thadities; this is Oak and this is Forthwind."

Oak was slowly getting over the shock of meeting a tree who was two distinct beings, but he thought, what's the difference between him and the dragons? None.

Oak extended his hand and shook Fielding's limb. Forthwind followed and then they both stood next to Thadities and waited.

Fielding asked for Thadities' patience while he told his tale. He then looked straight at Oak and Forthwind and said, "Oak and Forthwind's sire was a forester that worked in these wildwoods."

Oak looked at Forthwind and cried out, "What, what is this nonsense?"

Thadities looked down on Oak and said, "Silence, Oak. We will listen to Fielding's tale and then make a judgement."

The tree continued, "Rave was his name. His father, grandfather and great-grandfather were also foresters here in the wildwoods. Over many years he learned our secrets and wrote them down in a thick leather-bound book. Thousands of years were laid bare. We need that book found."

Oak and Forthwind looked at one another not quite trusting they were brother and sister. Oak knew they looked alike, but it would take a little time to realise he was not alone any longer; he had kin.

Forthwind took his hands in hers and said, "Brother."

Thadities asked Fielding, "Why does he need the book found? What is so dire that you drag us here to Welddpool without first asking for our help?"

Fielding held up a tree limb and begged once again for silence. "Rave and his wife, Adelina, were forced to flee their homeland, leaving their children behind. They fled by ship for another homeland because he fought every day for our survival and his enlightened ideals. For this loose talk they wanted to burn him at the stake for heresy.

"Now, there are men called the navigators near our shores who want to cut down the forests, for gold.

"We are home to many species of trees, rare plants and herbs. Many of these only grow on Welddpool. We have a few rare herbs that in the hands of good herbalists, would extend life for a short time, but we have heard tall tales grow around these herbs claiming they will extend life for hundreds of years. The greed of these men is unfathomable.

"If our secrets that Rave wrote down in his book should fall into the wrong hands, the navigators would wipe us off the face of the planet. Man would not survive. We have survived because man does not know we are alive. We have language, we sustain one another, and these characteristics must never be shared. Men would think it's magic and they would sell us to the highest bidder. It is not magic."

Fielding continued, "We need your power of flight, Thadities. We have help from the elementals, but they are too small and fragile to fly long distances and they are not strong enough to push the navigators back to where they came from."

Feilding looked straight at Thadities and said, "We had the assistance of your friend, Jerome in finding you."

"Jerome, the troll?" enquired Thadities.

"Yes," said Fielding. "He was the one who told us about your ancient legends concerning dragons and great knights fighting side by side in battles. We manipulated this story to entice you to Welddpool."

Thadities held his head in his talons and roared, "Jerome!" Silence.

"Are our kinsfolk alive?" he continued.

"Yes," said Fielding. "They are alive and are suspended in another dimension. They will not be harmed, and neither will they remember."

"Just one more thing before we leave, Fielding. What is an elemental?"

"They are forest dwellers and I will introduce you later. Now you, Oak and Forthwind have had enough surprises today and you need to re-join your clan and talk about our meeting."

They took their leave, and didn't stop until they reached camp, exhausted.

By the time Thadities had related the whole unbelievable tale, it was late, and they were exhausted. Tomorrow was a flight day, so goodnights were said, and silence greeted the trees that stood guard over them that night.

Chapter

# TEN

Next morning was fine and warm; a good flight day. The dragons lined up in their take off positions and they waited for a signal.

Oak climbed onto Thadities' neck and made himself comfortable. He placed the rope around his hand and looked around for Forthwind. She was aboard Grumpy.

The dragons' wings displaced the air, they hung suspended in the sky for a moment and then they were off.

Oak held onto the rope and breathed in the excitement that had shimmered in the air. Thadities spread his wings and then he slammed into a stronger gust of wind. It carried them higher and higher until Oak could barely breathe.

The clan kept up, and Grumpy had flown closer so Forthwind could be seen on his back, holding on tightly, as Oak remembered doing. Each dragon carried out its own flight manoeuvring. They all wove in and out, skimmed one another's wings tips but never touched. They were warriors.

He had noticed the clan had changed. Chalice had become the official clan leader, Steffen a code breaker and now Grumpy had come forward to be Forthwind's flight tutor and dragon ride. Daffadilly looked after the armoury and Oak's and Forthwind's training, and Waddle looked after them all. Those funny, elderly dragons had left and, in their place, now stood strong warriors.

What had changed for him? Having a sister was one huge change but how had he changed in other ways?

They flew over some ruins and then edged an ancient woodland he had never seen. They followed the course of a silent river until it emptied into the sea. Oak looked over Thadities' neck and saw the sea fall into nothingness. The sea was very scary Oak thought. He had been told a story about a knight who had crossed the sea and had never been seen again, just like his sire and mother. He wondered where they were or even if they were still alive.

Thadities and the clan had talked about their lives on their homeland. Their caves were built into the cliff faces, which looked out over the sea. Strange how men lived in different ways. He supposed everyone lived their lives as their ancestry dictated. He hoped after the quest and if they survived, he would be able to choose how he wanted to live.

Oak shook himself and looked around. No, he had not missed anything.

Thadities turned for home. He signalled Oak to be vigilant when they flew over the castle. There were no signs of life.

Thadities congratulated everyone on their return and said, "Tomorrow, before the sun rises to the centre of the sky, we must be ready to leave camp. Everything that is not needed will be returned to the castle and put in its rightful place. The camp will also be returned to the way we found it. Luckily, there was a tournament held at the castle a few days ago, so if the navigators come and look, all disturbances to the fields will blend into a confused mess."

"Where will we camp?" asked Oak.

"I have agreed to an area in the wildwoods that has been cleared for our occupation," said Thadities.

At sunrise, there was organised pandemonium. Oak and Forthwind were to-ing and fro-ing and got under everybody's talons. On their last trip to the castle they collected the hand cart and brought it into the camp.

As they entered camp Oak called to Thadities, "Have there been any changes?" He pointed to the maps that spilled out of their basket.

Thadities shook his head.

Oak placed the cart in the centre of the camp and it was soon full. A short time later the camp was bare; not a trace of them was to be seen.

Oak congratulated Waddle on a task well done.

"Thank you, Oak," she said. "I'm worried. When we return home, I don't want to go back to my old life and live in the retirement home for the elderly."

Oak looked into her concerned face and said, "Waddle, the quest will change everything for us all. You mustn't worry."

They shuffled into line and walked towards their destiny.

They obtained the fringe of the wildwoods with no trouble and Thadities took charge. "Tuck your wings close to your bodies; and you won't be scratched."

Thadities and Grumpy carried the children and entered the wildwoods first. The trees parted and allowed them safe passage. The crazy pathway was still and silent. They trod on the old adversary and were silenced and awed that the ancient wildwoods had allowed them within. The old trees stood sedentary with their limbs hanging straight against their trunks and nothing moved.

The pathway took a turn to the left and led them to a cleared area fit for a king. Food, water, plants and bedding awaited them there.

Oak leant down and said, "Thadities, no limbs pulled at us, no twigs or stones tripped us up, and not a murmured whisper was heard. Now, that's what I call a glorious way to be welcomed."

The clan settled in and watched with amazement when a messenger arrived from Fielding. It was tiny, and its wings moved so fast they were barely discernible. The dragons were terrified. The little being stood on Oak's head and introduced itself.

"My name is Adair and I am a nature spirit or an elemental, either title will do. We lived together with all magical beings once, until men found their way to our homeland. With your cruel beliefs, you drove the nature spirits underground and most other species have been destroyed. This place used to be known as 'Powers of Place' and it was once also our home. Fielding wanted us to meet."

Thadities welcomed Adair and said, "We show no disrespect, we just need to know where you are, so we don't squash you under our bulk."

Adair sat on Oak's head and pulled his hair as if he was holding onto a horse's reins. Thus, he led the clan to meet Fielding.

Fielding looked at the dragons closely for the first time. He had only met Thadities; all the other dragons had been at camp. His face changed colour as he asked, "Where are the warrior dragons? All I see are elderly dragons."

Thadities replied, "Fielding, these elderly dragons are my clan. They are a fierce group of dragons who have been prised out of retirement. Since our arrival they have trained and grown into a cohesive clan. Their outward accessories of eye wear, hearing trumpets and shawls must be overlooked because inside they are warriors."

Fielding bowed his limbs to the clan.

Chalice bowed to Fielding, and said, "We are elderly but well trained. All of us served our homeland well until we reached compulsory retirement age. Thadities is a fierce leader and warrior and under his command we will drive the enemy back over the waters."

Oak knew they were a clan of mismatched warriors; dragons who were both fierce and compassionate, trees that encompassed many species and then two fragile children with courageous hearts. What did Fielding really think of them all?

Nothing showed now on Fielding's face after he had met the clan.

Oak asked, "Will we do?"

Fielding replied, "You will do very well, thank you. Steffen, we thank you for your good work, it is imperative that Rave's book does not fall into the navigators' hands."

At that point, the ground shook all around them and large cracked areas appeared beneath the tree roots. They were much alarmed but before they gathered their wits about them, Oak ran towards Thadities, and shouted, "Thadities, Thadities... Look!"

When the ground shook the earth cracked and stairs had appeared.

Oak bounced over and peered into the darkness below. A black cavity yawned, and a stark silence greeted his ears, but undeterred, he crawled over the lip of the crack and slipped onto the first step. He fitted well into the indentation marked into the stone. He took a tentative second step and then a third. The dappled sunlight didn't penetrate that far, and as Oak allowed his eyes to adjust to the darkness a horrid, dank blackness oozed over his head, and disappeared into the light. What had brushed over him? Oak shuddered. He shot back up the steps and horror shone from everyone's faces.

Forthwind shouted, "Oak what was that, that...?"

"I have no notion of what it was," said Oak. "It just brushed past my head and disappeared into the light."

"Thadities," Fielding boomed. "Welcome to the Kingdom of Shadowland. We thought it would be more comfortable for you and the clan to live in the cavern instead of the camp, while we prepare for battle. While you reside at Shadowland every comfort will be shown to you in thanks for your generosity of spirt in agreeing to stay and fight."

Thadities bowed to Fielding and bellowed loudly, so the trees farthest away would hear him clearly. "I understand the menace that lurks on the high seas; these men called navigators, who have black hearts and minds that live in the swamps of evil. Our clan will endeavour to vanquish these men, so they will never take up arms again against any inhabitants of Welddpool. It will be our oath."

Every tree bowed, Oak and Forthwind cheered, and Chalice and Grumpy joined their oaths to Thadities' even though they had not been requested.

"When you have entered the tunnels of Shadowland, you will find such treasures hidden there. Many books live in their libraries. When the books were first brought into the wildwoods, trees, plants and elementals were unable to read any of the squiggly lines found scratched into the parchment, so they were just returned to the library shelves. Could Rave's book be hidden at Shadowland?" asked Fielding, with hope vibrating in his voice.

"Fielding, you have been a fierce adversary. Are all the trees as ferocious?" asked Thadities.

"Yes," replied Fielding. "There are many ancient trees amongst us who have fought many battles."

Thadities looked at Fielding in astonishment, and said, "I am being led to believe that the wildwoods can mount an attack on any intruders that had been stupid enough to cross the barrier, without permission. That the trees can coordinate an attack through their root system. You are a force so dangerous and malicious. Where do I start to learn?"

Fielding answered in a most reasonable tone, "Yes, we trees fight in our own way. Because we are stationary we are thought of as senile. The trees at the edge of the wildwoods watch, and message through their root system and disrupt anybody who has entered, uninvited. They are known as the co-operators."

Thadities asked, "Are there many species who have no language?"

"No, most have language. Underground, there is a system of tiny roots, linked to a number of species of fungi. These roots feed us, keep us healthy and in touch with our own kind and different species. Some trees are loners. It is far too complicated a system to discuss now, but we will talk about it another time," said Fielding.

Thadities said, "One more important question; the vortex. How does it work, and why was it wielded with such antagonism towards us?"

"That was a terrible mistake. The vortex sucked you in and the hawthorn was unable to close it down. Please accept our heartfelt apologies. I'll explain how it works later."

"The spiral tunnel is a weapon that could be used, if and when the navigators penetrate this far," said Thadities.

"Yes, if the navigators penetrate this far, a scent will be released by the trees and it will warn us they have breached our defences and attained our inner sanctum. The navigators will think the trees offer anonymity, but we don't. They will be watched and harshly punished. We are desperate to know where the navigators are camped. Our root system is decayed in places, some roots are missing so there are places that we are unable to reach. Could you and Oak start our alliance by a flight reconnaissance over the sea?"

"Of course," Thadities agreed. "When we return we will decamp to Shadowland. Oak, Forthwind and Steffen will then look for the book of Rave's."

Oak and Thadities left the wildwoods and returned to the field. They soared over the canopies and headed west. Their flight was uneventful and when Thadities and Oak looked towards the horizon they saw scores of galleons had sailed to the edge of the world, and there they sat, exposed in between the sea and sky. Thadities stopped mid-air, flexed his wings and brought them both about until Oak faced mounds of sand. Thadities' talons skimmed the tops and unsettled the grains, which cascaded every which way, but Thadities landed safely. Oak wondered if it was fun to be a dragon.

"That was fortunate, any farther out and we would have been seen by the navigators," he said. He pulled himself up over Thadities' lumps and bumps and stood on top of his head. He moved a telescope retrieved from the castle to his right eye and tried to count. Impossible. He slipped back down onto his indent and they scooted home.

"So, they are on the horizon. The navigators have sailed to our homeland. Our worst fears have come true," Fielding said, after he heard the navigators had been sighted. "Thadities, you and the clan can descend the steps into the underground caverns now. I have no memory of when the tunnel was last used but I am sure you are worthy of the adventure. The elementals have taken all your belongings from the camp site, and you will be met at the entrance to the great hall."

Oak and Forthwind descended into the darkness and were soon swallowed up. Grumpy, Steffen, Daffadilly, and Waddle descended next, and then Chalice and Thadities brought up the rear. Oak found the depth of the steps difficult, and so he placed his left hand on the wall and waited. He heard a stone slide into place and the steps were plunged into further darkness.

Oak heard the dragons as they scratched the stone with their nails, and he waited until the noise had died down before he moved forward. Oak soon encountered a wall sconce, set low in the rock, and to his joy there was an unlit taper. He pulled it towards him, called to Grumpy and asked, "Would you light the taper with your fire?"

"My flame is sparse and uncooperative since old age crept up on me, but I will try," said Grumpy.

Oak held the taper still and Grumpy took an experimental blow; it flared into life on his first attempt.

Oak, Forthwind and the dragons stood and glanced around the inky tunnel. It stank and was strewn with rotted vegetation and gigantic rats.

"Ugg," said Thadities. "I hate rats."

As they all moved forward, the water dripped down the rock face, ran over Oak's boots and into a channel set into the middle of the tunnel's floor. It smelt slimy and disgusting as it flowed into the darkness. Oak looked up towards the roof and saw hundreds of tiny roots were hung about the walls. They gave him the willies as they stared back at him. Oak picked up the pace and the ponderous dragons banged and slithered around behind him.

"Nooooo..." called out Daffadilly, as she slid down into slimy water. "A rat ran over my talon and I hate rats, pesky things."

Oak raised the lit taper and watched her skin change colour. She was embarrassed at her outcry and now she was blushing. Could anything else go wrong?

"Don't be worried now, Daffadilly. We'll help you," said Oak.

Thadities held her head still, and the clan heaved her upright. She wobbled about a bit but was soon strong enough to stand. Thadities brushed her down with averted eyes.

Forthwind asked, "Are you all right, Daffadilly?"

"Yes, I feel all sorts of a fool but I'm unhurt. How are you doing Forthwind? You're very quiet lately."

"There is much to be learned. I watch and listen to the dragons, and now I feel more at ease around you. Also, Grumpy's flight lessons have created a strong bond and now he treats me as a warrior instead of a lady's maid," she replied.

"The last time we were at the castle, you had a longbow. Where is it now?" asked Daffadilly.

"It was hidden at camp and I hope the elementals found it and took it to the cavern. No one but you has asked about the longbow. Why's that?" asked Forthwind.

"I believe you haven't told the whole truth about your mastery over many weapons, which include the longbow. Am I right?" asked Daffadilly.

Oak and Daffadilly looked at Forthwind but before she could answer there was a shout from Thadities.

Oak turned and saw the end of the tunnel had turned blue. Oak slipped and slid on the stone floor as he approached the light, but he saw that it blazed from a smaller tunnel on his left. Oak smelt the air and said, "This air is not tainted; the tunnel has been cleaned and the blue orbs cast a welcome light."

Thadities came to the front and scooped Oak and Forthwind up with his talons. "Oak, you've displayed a courageous willingness towards many challenging tasks over the last few days and you have grown into a tough knight-in-training. We dragons are honoured to serve with you."

Oak beamed, glanced at Forthwind and scrambled up Thadities' neck. He could barely contain his glee.

The dragons huddled together and shuffled down towards the blue light. A door was opened, and an elemental beckoned them inside and said, "My name is Ackerley, please follow me." They walked down a short corridor and were soon shown into a beautiful room.

"Oh!" they all gasped as they found themselves inside a large, warm room. The room had a high domed ceiling with twinkling crystals set in blue plaster moulds. The polished wood floor was pristine, so they gingerly walked into its centre and waited for their guide to speak.

"Refreshments will be found on the oval table over there," he said as he pointed to the furthest wall. "Adair sends his apologies. He has been held up over a matter of homeland security and has asked that you make yourselves comfortable while you wait."

Nodding, he left the room, closing the door softly behind him.

Oak and Forthwith got down off Thadities' back and darted into every corner.

Finally, they shouted, "Thadities!" He looked down and saw them sitting on tiny chairs.

"Stop!" Thadities called a halt to their madness. Everyone froze, turned and looked at Thadities.

"We'll eat while we are waiting for Adair," Thadities said.

The food was glorious, so they stuffed themselves until they were barely able to move and then Oak and Forthwind found a comfy spot in the middle of a large chair and drifted off to sleep.

Chapter

# ELEVEN

Who pulled my ear? Oak wondered. He sat up, rubbed his eyes in disbelief at the sight before him. "Who are you?"

"Shari. I'm a nature spirit," she replied, as she flapped her wings all around Oak's face.

Oak sat bolt upright and tried to grab her with one hand, but she just giggled and moved her gossamer wings beyond his reach.

"Here's another one!" Oak shouted out to the clan.

Shari had flown up towards Thadities' head and she perched herself at the end of his nose. "Are you Thadities?" she asked.

Without waiting for an answer, she stood up and launched herself out of the room.

"Yes," he replied, as he followed her with his nose in the air. The rest of the dragons wanted to play the same game and shot their noses in the air before they left the room.

"Oh!" Oak gasped, as he spied a hole where the ceiling should have been. An inky darkness peered down at him. It was peppered with twinkling stars and a small diminished moon, but his attention was soon drawn to the room's far wall, which was hung with hundreds of dull quartz crystal points.

A voice trickled out of the murk, and said, "The quartz crystals are used to store the consciousness of every tree, plant and fungus that lives on this homeland. They are guarded by the elementals day and night. Down in the depths of the cavern we have had a theft, and a few are missing, causing some of the tree roots to be disconnected. This is a danger to the wildwoods while they are under threat. This is why I was unable to greet you when you arrived. I was trying to calm the roots down."

The voice continued, "By daybreak Shadowland's libraries will have been cleaned and ready to be occupied by you. Now, as it is so late, you will be shown to your sleeping rooms." An elemental appeared out of the gloom. He was no stranger, Oak realised, but the same elemental they had met in the clearing. He came forward and took Thadities' talon into his little hand and pumped it up and down.

"Hello Adair," said Oak.

The elemental turned to smile at him. "You remembered my name! I am Shari's father and one of the elders of the elementals," he said. "Now, it's too late for niceties." He clapped his hands and brought forth an elemental who asked the clan to follow him.

"What exactly is an elemental?" Oak asked Shari as they left the room.

"We're nature spirits," she replied.

"What are nature spirits?" Oak asked.

"Little folk. Once, long ago, men and the magical world of the unknown all lived together in harmony. Then, deliberately, our way of life was eroded by men who wanted to dominate or destroy everything in their path, and that included us. Mankind's greed had no limits, so we were forced to move underground and live our lives in the shadows. That's why our home is called Shadowland."

"Are there many of your kind?" asked Thadities, who had been listening.

"Yes," Shari replied. "The elementals have thrived, and the ancient root language has kept us connected to Fielding and other displaced folk."

Shari stepped inside a set of double doors and the clan followed. Oak saw the sleeping quarters had been cut into the rocks and were large, warm and dry. Thadities turned to Shari and said, "Thank you, we've been welcomed very warmly and now it's time to say goodnight."

Shari left, and a guard was placed outside for their protection. The dragons and the children plonked themselves down on the floor and slept.

Chapter

# TWELVE

Oak and Forthwind poked their noses out of their quarters in the morning and saw the guard across the hallway. He left his post and they were shown to the great hall, while the dragons were led down a back tunnel to where fresh greenery was served.

After their morning meal, Shari took Oak, Forthwind and Steffen into a beautiful library that was lined with hundreds of leather bound books, ranged by size. They all looked heavy to Oak.

Shari had flown around the room twice and then she dived towards a book which hung over the edge of one of the top shelves. She glanced at the spine and called down, "Oak would you slide the ladder underneath? I've found the book I wanted."

Oak slid the ladder into place and leant towards the shelves. As he reached for the red leather-bound book, the gold lettering on its spine jiggled up and down. Startled, he dropped the book and it spreadeagled across the wooden floor. He slid down the ladder, jumped the last rung, scooped the book up and ran over to Shari.

"Move over," he said, and he sat down. Shari had flown onto the top of the table and opened the book to its first page. Oak peered at the page with a puzzled frown. What book was this?

Shari said, "Oak, Forthwind, you know your father was a woodsman and the trees revealed their history and their language to him. He was an enlightened man for his time, and when he realised the trees had a language he made a connection with Fielding and they became friends.

"When Rave and Adelina were forced to flee, he and the nature spirits collected all the books they could find and brought them to Shadowland where they have lived on the library shelves ever since. The book Fielding seeks has never been found because we can't read, but the squiggles on the spine of this book have always jumped around so I have always wondered if it was special."

Shari beckoned Oak and Forthwind to climb upon the table so that they could read the words and check to see if they were placed there by Rave, their father. Oak climbed onto the table, reached for the book and pulled it towards him.

His father's hand had written these words. He traced them with his finger and tears dripped unheeded down his face. Forthwind leant over, dabbed at his tears and they both read his words.

*I write these words so that one day my children, Oak and Forthwind, will be shown my written journal.*

*My name is Rave, and I worked most of my life as a woodsman. I and another worked the main wildwoods. I knew I was being watched, and when it was time for the trees to be thinned, there was such malevolence in the air and I was afraid. Over time I discovered many magical things about the trees and wildwoods. I wrote down their magic but never spoke about the secret lives of the trees, because my kinsfolk would have called me mad and brayed for my death at the stake, with the charge of heresy ringing in my ears.*

*Time passed, and I and the trees got to know more and more about each other until eventually Fielding felt it was time we left the district and Welddpool for our own safety. Your mother Adelina and I packed our belongings, and we had to make the heartbreaking decision to leave you both behind because we were unable to secure safe passage for us all to sail together to a distant land. We placed you both with old family retainers and if you are reading these I thank the saints, you have survived.*

Steffen asked Shari, "Did Rave keep a diary?"

"I don't know, he may have," she replied.

Steffen carefully replaced the book onto the shelf where it had lived since Rave disappeared. Shari opened a connecting door to reveal another beautiful room. Oak skidded to a halt just inside the room when he spied the largest tapestry he had ever seen. Beautiful colours gleamed from an intricately woven pattern of scenes taken from nature.

Oak asked Shari, "Was this your land? The ancients with their strong belief in magic and community must have had their souls destroyed when man first appeared."

"They are still called the destroyers; they have never learnt anything. To rape and pillage the land for timber, rare plants and herbs was always their goal, but this time they brought added danger with them."

Shari stopped speaking. Oak waited.

Adair, Thadities and the clan entered the room. Under the tapestry was a high round table and several chairs. Oak looked at these and was dismayed; if Thadities and the other dragons sat on those dainty chairs they would splinter the wood and end up sprawled on the floor.

Adair had flown into the centre of the room and said, "A large room has been allocated for the dragons' use and if they follow me I will show them the way."

Steffen then interrupted the flow and told the assembled clans that they had found Rave's leather-bound book. Shari had had an idea the book was important, and it was. The room erupted. Everybody wanted to know How? When? Where? Thadities called for calm and shouted, later... later they would have all the questions answered but not now.

"Thank you, Adair, please carry on," said Thadities, and they all followed Adair down a short corridor they had not been in before and entered a huge room.

Oak and Forthwind stood in the centre and the dragons arranged themselves on the outer rim and Thadities said, "Tomorrow morning as the sun rises, I and Oak, Forthwind and Grumpy, Chalice and Adair and Daffadilly and Shari will take separate flight paths. We will then have covered all of the homeland in one swoop. Oak will be my eyes, Forthwind will be Grumpy's, Adair will be Chalice's, and Shari will be Daffadilly's. We will have two special harnesses made by tonight so Adair and Shari are safely attached to their dragons."

Thadities swung his intelligent gaze around everyone, nodded his head, and asked for questions.

Oak raised his hand and said, "Thadities?" as his gaze drifted over the assembled clan.

The dragon turned to him.

"How detailed do you want our observations to be? Most of us are novices and tiny in stature. No offence to anybody here, but I have peered over Thadities' head many times and it's difficult to do."

Thadities looked at the nature spirits, and said, "Each harness will attach you to the back of the dragon's necks. Some protection from the wind will be offered and you will be able to scan the horizon and the terrain below you and note any changes." He turned to the spirit elder. "How many warriors are at your command?"

"Over one thousand men, women and children. All are trained and ready," replied Adair, and he chuckled at their surprise.

"Oak, you come with me," said Thadities.

Everyone else slowly left the room, and Forthwind and Steffen went to study Rave's notes. They needed to know what he had written down about the life of the trees and plants. Oak followed Thadities down into a maze of tunnels and he saw thousands more roots hung around the ceilings and walls, their tips glowing. They were alive, as Oak noted in surprise.

"Oak, we don't understand a thing yet, so you and the clan just need to keep your months shut and listen," said Thadities. "We won't cause any upset, but I want you to be on your guard until we know more about these mysterious navigators."

Oak left Thadities and eventually found himself back in the library with Forthwind and Steffen. He wanted to see his sire's handwriting again; it brought him closer somehow.

Clang! went a bell, so the trio packed away the book and went and searched for the great hall. As Oak entered the hall, he noticed that the dragons' greenery had been brought to one side of the room. Kindness, he thought; now they don't have to eat in the old tunnel.

Adair brought the noisy hall quickly to order and said, "The elementals have a rule that nobody talks during meal times. Discussion does not aid digestion; silence does."

Chapter

# THIRTEEN

After they had supper eaten they all shuffled out of the great hall and within a short time were back together again; this time in the meeting room.

Thadities asked Chalice and Daffadilly to come forward and he placed the harnesses around their heads. Thadities asked Daffadilly to bend her neck. She bent her neck and her eyewear slid down and bumped her nose.

"Oh, not again," she shouted.

Adair clapped his hands and a couple of nature spirits entered the room. "Go and find me some grasses that have a little flexibility left so that we can manipulate the plant into a plait." They bowed and left the room.

They returned with handfuls of grasses and Shari sat and made a plait long enough to go around Daffadilly's head and neck.

Thadities threaded the plait through Daffadilly's eyewear and anchored it behind her neck. She beamed back at Thadities and said, "I am now ready for anything. With my anchored eyewear and Shari's harness hung just at the right spot at the back of my neck I will be a formidable scout. Perfect."

It had been a long day. Goodnights were said, and the clan went to their sleeping quarters. Oak was too wound up to sleep and just laid his head on Thadities' rump and counted the hours before the sun rose.

"Oak," called Forthwind out of the darkness. "Should I have my longbow with me tomorrow?"

Oak replied, "Yes, you should have your weapon; what would happen if we were stranded and had to find our own way back?"

Forthwind left the sleeping quarters and went and searched for her longbow. She found it in the armoury and returned with it in her hand with a full complement of arrows.

They slept and Thadities woke them to darkness. "Ready, Oak, Forthwind?"

"Ready, Thadities," said Oak. He put on his armour and placed his sword into his waistband. All the while he ate the bread he had saved from supper last evening to save time.

Something screeched. Oak jumped and wondered where the noise had come from. He looked towards the end of the tunnel and saw a circle of stone had slid back into a recess. They walked towards the shards of muted moonlight that speared the darkness and found themselves in an open field. Over to their right a copse of trees stood guard.

Thadities flexed his wings and they were off into a cold unwelcoming sky. Oak was very thankful he had on his warm undergarments.

He turned his head and watched the other dragons as they took off to carry out their missions. Adair and Shari, safe in their harnesses, were invisible to the naked eye, but he knew they were strapped onto the backs of the dragons somewhere.

Thadities had flown straight towards the sun as it rose from its bed, hit a head wind and veered to his left. Oak held on and marvelled at his improved mastery since the start of his flight lessons. Oak saw no movement underneath, and soon Thadities sailed over the cliffs and as Oak looked down he saw many abandoned wooden boats. Most had been dragged up onto the beach and left there. Odd, thought Oak, there were no fires burning, and no lookouts posted. Thadities turned around and zig zagged along the shore and then moved inland slightly, while all the while Oak looked for the navigators.

Thadities lifted his head and Oak tightened the rope around his hand. Had he received a telepathic message from one of the other dragons? Oak mused to himself that there were many ways of fighting this enemy. The dragons could send and receive messages though they were hundreds of miles apart, and the elementals and the trees had this mastery as well. They could ambush the navigators from beneath and above the ground, and from the sky. This quest would be won because men thought they were gods and invincible and they were not.

On their return flight, Oak spied an unknown knoll and made a mental note to ask Thadities why he'd flown so far out of their area. Apart from this anomaly the flight home was uneventful. They joined the clan at the entrance to the tunnel. Thadities frowned.

Thadities called out to Adair as they reached the corridor, "Oak and I checked the knoll and it was denuded of life, a wasteland. Down at the beach, many boats have been dragged up above the water line, but no fires were burning and no lookouts posted. Why have the navigators abandoned their boats and disappeared? Something is very wrong here."

Heads bounced up and down, as if in agreement that something was very wrong indeed.

Thadities looked up and said, "I felt Oak and I were not observed, and nothing below us moved. I have no leads on where the navigators are holed up, but we must go back tonight when it's dark and scuttle their boats."

They made their way to the meeting room, and when they were all settled Adair asked the other assembled dragons what else they had seen.

Chapter

# FOURTEEN

Forthwind raised her hand and asked to speak. "I saw a large tract of grass flattened between two stands of trees. Grumpy and I flew no further because the clouds parted, and we felt exposed."

"Grumpy," asked Thadities, "which direction was that?"

"We flew north east, and the field was a couple of miles inland from the Cliffs of Dale," replied Grumpy.

"Adair, do you have a map of the island? I had a couple at camp but have lost them."

A map was produced and spread out over the table that had been hastily dragged into the command room by Oak and Forthwind. Adair pointed to the location of the Cliffs of Dale, and said, "They protect an inlet about five miles across from the main beach where Thadities and Oak saw the abandoned boats. That explains why they didn't see any trace of the navigators. They walked across the beach and not inland."

Thadities enquired, "Adair, what lies beyond that stretch of grass?"

"Ruins. An old abandoned castle," he replied, as he pointed to the map.

There were no further comments from the other dragons. Their flights had been uneventful. Everybody started to drift away towards the great hall and Thadities said, "Today, the clan showed me how adept they are at coping with their many new and varied responsibilities. Before my eyes they've become a cohesive clan of scouts and warriors."

They blushed, blubbered and were incoherent with their praise for one another, but mostly they all stood tall and beamed back at Thadities. Oak wished he could draw. What a story that would have told!

Soon after, Oak and Forthwind tucked into their food. They relished the freshness of the bread, the tang of the meat and the sweetness of the milk. Thadities and the clan were served fresh greens. The clan had never been so well looked after and Thadities thanked Adair for his continued generosity.

"You are the light that has been called upon to shine on our darkest hour, and I want to salute you," Adair responded. He then disappeared into the corridor.

A bell sounded all around the cavern. Thadities and the clan left the great hall and gathered once again in the meeting room and waited.

Adair had summonsed his elemental guards and they flew into the room and joined them. They gave a collective nod to Thadities but focused their eyes on Adair. "Guards, you must make a long journey to the main beach and Thadities' orders will be obeyed," Adair said.

They nodded and flew from the room. The clan strode to the tunnel entrance and the guards clambered aboard

Thadities and held onto anything they could find, including Oak. Once they were secure he made the slow and perilous journey towards the sea.

As Thadities and Oak approached the sand dunes, Oak spied the clan and elemental guards hidden by a fringe of stunted trees on the edge of the dunes. "They've arrived before us," Oak shouted to Thadities.

They gathered on the foreshore of the beach. Thadities and Oak, Forthwind and Grumpy assembled teams of nature spirits and started to pull the boats towards the sea. It was dark, the moon had not risen yet, and the boats were heavy. Somebody was going to get hurt. To avert disaster, Oak shouted out, "Stop."

They stopped.

"Right, the dragons can't pull or drag the boats into the water, but once there, they can pulverise them into sticks. Forthwind and I will thread a rope through the metal ring at the front of the boats and with the help of the nature spirits we can pull and push the boats into the shallow water. Thadities and Adair do not want the boats destroyed on the sand."

Oak threaded a rope through the metal ring and the first boat was half dragged and pushed into shallow water. Thadities and the dragons placed their talons into the boat and pushed down.

Creak, crash! It splintered into millions of pieces. Nobody came to investigate the noise.

The three different clans worked together throughout the night until the last boat was scuttled. Oak and the nature spirts jumped aboard Thadities and reviewed their night's work. His heart soared as they turned towards the cavern as the sky lightened. Their mission had been successful.

Before they set off, Thadities let the guards know he and Oak had been asked to visit the wildwoods and they could fly back to Shadowland from there. As they approached the hedge two trees parted and showed them the pathway. Thadities and

Oak stepped onto the path and it twisted, turned and wound its way through the trees until they found themselves back at the edge of the woodland. Thadities scratched his head with a talon and looked about him.

Oak then saw the trees were crying silently, and their sap had pooled at their base of their trunks. Nasty.

"The navigators have not entered the wildwoods," Oak said.

They returned to the cavern and Adair delivered a message from Fielding. "Don't be alarmed, the wildwoods have on their battle armour today and were practising their defence against the navigators."

Adair congratulated them on their success and they adjourned to the great hall.

After their morning meal the clan gathered around their circle and Thadities spoke. "Tonight, Chalice, Grumpy and I will find the old ruins."

The day was their own. They caught up with some sleep and practised with their weapons until supper.

After supper, the three dragons left the tunnel and were watched until they disappeared into the gloom.

Oak was unsettled so he went to find Adair. "Do you have any rags? I want to polish my armour."

They were quickly found, and Oak returned to the main room. He diligently polished his breast plate and kept his worrying thoughts to himself. He had worn a courageous face all evening and that was all he needed to do.

Oak let out a sigh and as he looked up, he suddenly grinned from ear to ear. They were home!

"What do you have in your talon, Thadities?" shouted out Daffadilly.

Thadities moved past the clan and placed a small wooden box on the table. They all crowded around and peered down as Thadities lifted the lid slowly and revealed tree roots. They were showing signs of damage, but their points glowed and cast eerie shadows onto the interior of the little box.

Baffled faces turned towards him and he said, "Roots, tree roots."

Adair told them these were called antennas and they worked with the crystals that hung in the shadow room. They sent all the messages used by the different tribes that shared his homeland.

The room erupted, and everybody babbled at once. Thadities had to shout to be heard.

"Silence," he yelled. "I flew straight to the old ruins. It was abandoned a long time ago, and is in a disreputable state of repair, but it glowed from the inside. Chalice and I flew higher and hid amongst the darkening clouds. Chalice noticed there were boxes scattered over the dirt track. She swooped down and retrieved one box without being seen. We both flew over the castle and saw the navigators. They were drunk and had posted no lookouts anywhere along the road or inside the ruins."

Adair approached Thadities' talons and took the box. He held it with reverence and spoke to the contents in a low humming tone. The roots responded by a slight movement of their tips. Shari ran over and joined them in the oddest conversation Oak had ever heard.

Then he thought; he spoke to the dragons in a different language, they both spoke to the nature spirits in a different one again, so why not have a third for the roots? Did he have the knowledge to speak to the roots?

Adair had spoken to the roots; what had they told him?

Adair said, "Many have tried and failed over the years, to find these mythical herbs. Now Fielding thinks the navigators must have heard some of the old tales that have been around for years, about the magic properties of these rare herbs and had come to find them even if it meant destroying the wildwoods. Now, finding the roots in their possession supports this belief.

The roots have not shared all their secrets even with the elementals of Wilddpool. How do the navigators hope to get them to share their secrets with them? Do you think they have heard about Rave's book?"

Oak stood about and waited for Adair to be alone, but Shari approached him first. "Oak," she called shyly. "Come, we've decided that we are going to read Rave's writings."

She led him out of the room and down into the main library. Forthwind and Steffen sat at the main table waiting patiently for him to join them.

Forthwind said, "Oak, he wrote many words to describe the secret world of trees and fungi. The roots are the lifeforce of the trees; they provided them with food, water and language. They even look after them when they are sick. The trees release an invisible mist into the air to ward off predators and they let the other trees know of any danger lurking about. He has written where the rare herbs are to be found and how to use them. He has revealed too many secrets about the trees."

Forthwind turned to the last page and continued, "Rave has written about a family curse that runs through the male line only. It affects their bones while they are growing and when they have reached adulthood, the pain disappears. Our father wished his male descendants be told."

Forthwind glanced over at Oak and he placed his finger over his lips for silence.

Steffen said, "Now they knew, not magic, just the way the wildwoods had evolved over the centuries. Man could get very rich from the timber, herbs and plants found in these wildwoods, but their expectation of longevity was nonsense."

"Could we explain to men, who saw only gold, that there was a higher reason to leave the wildwoods be? No, they would not listen."

They shuffled out of the room, Steffen shut the door behind them and they walked straight into another uproar.

Adair flew past with the box in his hands with Thadities right behind.

"What's happened now?" said Oak.

An unwanted entourage then accompanied Adair as he left the corridor. By the time he arrived at the forbidden tunnel they were all still on his tail. Fortunately, the dragons were too big and cumbersome to enter the small tunnel. Adair was swallowed up by the darkness and they leant up against the ancient walls and waited.

"Augh, Ah, Ode," they heard from deep inside the tunnel.

"What was that?" said Thadities, as he peered into the darkness.

Shari explained, "The roots are traumatised, and Adair has welcomed them back into the fold."

Adair reappeared and nodded.

Adair confronted Thadities after he'd returned to the meeting room. "Thadities, a thief lives amongst us. The box you found on the road to the ruins carried the roots taken from the tunnel. The boxes you left behind might have also carried roots because there are a few more missing. The thief will be found and sentenced. The navigators must be kept in ignorance about this find. At dark, two scouts will be posted inside one of the arrow slits on the front battlements of the ruins. They will keep a look out for the missing roots. They will leave shortly, so if you have any last orders, let them know."

Adair clapped his hands and a nature spirt arrived and sat on Thadities' nose.

Oak laughed out loud and waited for Thadities to react. He's so tiny, Oak thought, but he has greater agility than the dragons or even me.

"Have you a name?" asked Thadities.

"I am called Thorn," he replied.

Thadities asked, "How experienced are you in reconnaissance?"

"Very experienced," Thorn replied.

"Well then, you don't need me to stick my nose in your affairs," said Thadities.

Thorn bowed to the room in general and was gone.

"Adair, we weren't able to leave the homeland when we tried. The web and force field were too strong. Are the structures very complex? They seem unfathomable to me."

"The sky's web and the vortex work on separate root systems. The roots under Shadowland work on a different system because they run from a separate stand of trees. Each species is connected to its own kind, and some species work harmoniously with different species and even more are independent. You will not be shown how the roots work at this time, just know that when it comes to the penetration of the woodland you won't be alone," Adair replied as he shooed them all to their sleeping quarters.

Adair then went to tell Fielding about the content of Rave's book.

Chapter

# FIFTEEN

The next morning after a good night's sleep, Oak joined his fellow warriors and sidled up to Daffadilly. She looked over her eye wear and grinned.

"Good morning, Oak," Daffadilly said.

"Good morning," he replied. "Daffadilly, you've shown me more affection than any of the castle kinsfolk since I was taken in and I want to say thanks."

Daffadilly ruffled his hair and gave no thought to how her nails scratched his scalp.

Oak moved away in case blood dripped onto his vest. He wouldn't want her to be hurt, as she was so kind.

Eventually, everybody was settled and ready for the morning's talk. When Thadities arrived, he carried old parchment and maps. Oak sighed and settled more deeply into the oversized chair.

Thadities cleared his throat and said, "Fielding sent his grateful thanks and he will leave the book here, until the quest is over. He knew Rave had written down dangerous secrets about the trees and plants. If the navigators enter Shadowland, the elementals know how to burn the book, also the standing stones have been hidden."

Bang! went the door as it was torn off its hinges, and in stomped the ugliest man Oak had looked upon. He was tall and stood around the height of Thadities' shoulder. Thadities and he looked each other up and down and then they both roared with laughter. The giant placed his arms around Thadities and gave him a squeeze. Thadities let out the funniest noise Oak had ever heard. Was he pleased?

"Jerome," shouted Thadities. "Why are you here?"

"I passed through the invisible corridor on my way home, glanced over and saw you and wondered why my friend was in Shadowland," replied Jerome.

"Our kinsfolk vanished, and, driven by an old legend, we arrived on Welddpool to look for two mythical great knights. We found Oak and tried to go home and were defeated. He then told us about his kinsfolk vanishing and shortly after Forthwind was found. Now pay attention because the oddest part of the story unfolds now. A tree, whose name is Fielding by the way, told me about a troll called Jerome and how he helped them to exploit an old legend of ours."

"Oh," said Jerome. "Sorry, when I found out they needed help I let Fielding know about our friendship, and how, over the centuries, you have helped us repel many enemies. Then I told him about your connection to the great knights of Welddpool and that must be why you have found yourselves in such a pickle. How can I put it right?"

"We desperately need help to guard Pembrokeshire Castle. There is far too much armoury and weaponry inside its walls to be left unguarded."

"Righty-o," said Jerome. "I and my homeland owe you much gratitude that stretches back for centuries."

Jerome gave those assembled the once over, sniffed and went and stood near Grumpy.

"Clan," said Thadities. "This is Jerome. He hails from a homeland called Ceres. Between us, we've overpowered many greedy enemies over the centuries, just because they thought Ceres' abundance of treasures were there for them to plunder and live off the yield. Dragons fought alongside the trolls as we used to fight alongside men."

Jerome left then, and Oak presumed he went to fetch more trolls.

Fielding and Adair closeted themselves together in the meeting room and asked not to be disturbed. Daffadilly, Oak and Forthwind spent the day checking all their weaponry and equipment. It had not been checked since they had entered Shadowland and it was an important job that had been left for too long. By the end of a long and arduous day they found nothing was amiss and every piece was accounted for.

The clan then turned in for the night and Oak now understood that they would hold their first council of war in the morning.

Chapter

# SIXTEEN

Thump, thump.

Oak opened one eye and saw Jerome with a detached door in his hand.

"Sorry," he said, as he looked down at the lump of timber dangling in his hand. Embarrassed, he propped the door against the wall and looked around for Thadities. They soon left the room together without a word being uttered.

Oak and Forthwind spend the morning honing their mastery over their weapons and later, Shari showed them both into a room they had never entered. Oak stood on a patterned square stone and was mesmerised. What was this room's history? Thadities asked them all to come closer so he could be heard.

The trolls and the nature spirits seemed to have an infinity with each other, so they stood together. Oak and Forthwind sat with the dragons and they all turned to look at Thadities, their natural leader.

Thadities stood in front of a pile of parchment and as he searched through it, he said, "Jerome has brought back a unit of foot soldiers. They will be billeted at the castle and Adair has called for volunteers to be their scouts.

"Jerome, these are my warriors," he continued as he glanced over at the assembled clan. "Oak is a knight-in-training and Forthwind is a longbow woman. Steffen is a scholar and warrior, Chalice is our coordinator and Daffadilly our armourer."

Thadities paused for breath and continued, "Grumpy is our flight master and Forthwind's dragon and Waddle is our camp coordinator. Adair, Shari and the elementals you know."

Jerome bowed and looked at Oak before he said, "Oak, you lived at the castle?"

"Yes, it was my home," Oak replied. "Forthwind and I need heavier garments and if Thadities gives us both permission, we will be your guides." Oak looked over at Thadities and permission was given.

Oak led the trolls out of the chamber, through a maze of tunnels and into a cool breeze. The trolls picked up their clubs from the tunnel's entrance and then they were off.

Nasty weapons, Oak thought. Wicked iron nails had been hammered into their surfaces and were so discoloured Oak wondered if they were still stained by dried blood.

Jerome stopped and bent down before Oak and said he wanted to see Fielding again before they continued on to the castle.

Oak and Forthwind nodded, turned to their right and walked through a field of night stars; they were very pretty but nobody stopped to take notice. They continued due east until they reached the fringe of the wildwoods. The trolls spread themselves out along the tree line, but they were powerless against the hedge. Oak had not realised the trolls had fallen behind, so as he turned he watched fascinated as the tree limbs crept along the ground, fastened onto the trolls' legs and pulled them to their knees. The woodland floor moaned; had it been hurt?

Oak ran to the trolls. "What happened?" Then he yelled as the tree limbs gave him a nasty bite. He shouted out, "Something is very odd here, so don't antagonise the trees any further."

He left them where they lay and ran through the woodlands. The pathway allowed him to find Fielding quickly.

"Fielding," Oak called. "The trolls have come to defend the castle and the tree limbs have attacked them. Why?"

Fielding looked angry and said, "Oak, a catastrophe has happened. The navigators prowled around outside the wildwood's fringe last night and banged iron nails into their trunks. These trees are hurt, and they need to be helped, now."

Oak ran and called to Forthwind, "The tree limbs will now unravel."

Oak and Forthwind helped Jerome and as he sat on his bottom he looked most put out. Oak explained that the navigators had driven nails into the trees last night and they needed to be removed quickly. Could he help?

Oak and Forthwind removed the last of the tree limbs from the soldiers and the limbs slithered across the ground back to their masters. Sap oozed out of the holes when the nails were removed but it dried when it smelt the air, and it left no mark behind. Not a sound was heard.

The trees bowed their thanks as the trolls decided to return to Shadowland.

"Thadities," Oak called, as he neared the entrance to the main tunnel.

Thadities thundered out of the tunnel, and Oak threw himself at his leg and asked that he bend down.

"The navigators have hammered iron nails into several tree trunks near the hedge. Jerome and his soldiers think they've removed them all," Oak said in a breathless voice.

Thadities looked at Jerome and said he'd heard that old wives' tale; nails that had been hammered into tree trunks kept evil away. The navigators must be very afraid of what they might encounter in the wildwoods.

"Jerome, it's way past the time we should visit the ruins. Can you stay here and send your soldiers to take up residence in the castle before it's too late?" said Thadities.

Oak and Forthwind found themselves, once again, on the road to the castle. Forthwind needed to practise with her longbow, so she aimed and hit many of the trolls' clubs as they swung back and forth and mimicked their master's strides. They thought she was a great shot. Oak thought she was a show off.

Earlier, Grumpy had flown ahead, and they now knew the castle had not been overrun by the navigators. Without warning, the trolls picked up Oak and Forthwind and carried them back to the castle. Oak thought the dragons smelt, but the trolls were even worse.

The day had crossed over with the night, and it was time they left. Oak and Forthwind had enjoyed their time with the trolls. Oak had not realised how funny they were, so he was sad to leave them behind. Both Oak and Forthwind climbed aboard Grumpy and the dragon arched his wings, displaced the cold air, and they were off. They waved until their arms were sore.

When they landed Thadities took off and they saw Jerome running in the distance. Oak watched until he was a speck in the sky and then he belted down the tunnel and looked for Steffen. He spied him in the corner of the largest library and said, "Have they still gone to the ruins?"

"Yes, and they won't be long," replied Steffen. Before the words were out of his mouth Thadities and Jerome had returned. They heard them as they clattered through the hallways. They left the library together and went and joined them.

Thadities looked excited and he said, "Clan, it has begun."

There were many raised hands but before anyone asked a question regarding what had begun, a nature spirit was paraded into the room. He was pulled up in front of Adair and he went on one knee and begged for forgiveness.

Adair spluttered, "Why? why?..."

"Why? I did it for gold. I am envious of my friends who have more gold then me. I just wanted to belong. Without gold in your pockets they look down on you with pity in their eyes, so I sold some roots to a trader in the outside markets. I embellished a tale about the fundamental magic found in tree roots and he believed me. I've no idea why they were found on the track or even if the navigators know any were dropped. That is the only lot I sold," cried the nature spirit, whose name was still unannounced.

Adair looked him up and down and saw the terror that lurked behind his eyeballs. It was decided that he would be placed under cavern arrest. The man was relieved, and he deflated like a pricked bladder as he waited to be escorted out of the room.

Adair explained later that not to mention an elemental's name was the highest insult in the homeland.

"Now it's time for us to move back to the wildwoods. We will leave shortly, so be ready when you're called," said Thadities. "I will assign tasks as soon as I have spoken to Fielding."

They negotiated their way back through the tunnels and noticed the roots were very agitated. Up the wide steps they plodded and found the stone cover had been removed. They were greeted by a sickly moon and a few stars.

On the way back to camp Oak thought the woods were hushed and secretive. "Thadities, Fielding might want us back in the wildwoods, but do the wildwoods want us to?"

"We will tackle in the morn any unease that has arisen from the navigators' attempts to unsettle the wildwoods. I felt the distress that clung to the trees, but Fielding expects us to move back into camp. All will be well, Oak," Thadities said, as he patted his back.

The call to visit Fielding did not arrive and so they waited. The frosts were hostile, and the ground was hard but Fielding wanted them to be living in the wildwoods when the summons came. Oak and Forthwind practised their mastery over their weapons and kept as warm as they could.

On the morn of the second day a rolled-up parchment was found. Oak never found out who had left it.

Thadities shouted, "At last, the navigators have moved camps. Fielding and the wildwoods have summoned us to a gathering."

Oak and Forthwind dressed. Oak's armour felt heavy and uncomfortable and he was uneasy within himself. He looked over at Forthwind and saw her skin was drained of colour. No words were spoken, and they followed Thadities out of the camp. The travelled along unfamiliar pathways until they come across an area of flattened grass. Thadities stopped, placed his ear against an oak tree, turned and said, "Wait." He and Grumpy disappeared into the wildwoods.

Oak prowled around and was tempted to travel further afield but didn't quite have the courage to ignore Thadities' orders. The weak sun had travelled to the centre of the sky and had started its slow descent before Thadities returned with Grumpy just behind.

"Oak, Forthwind; climb aboard."

They moved in unison and grappled with their cumbersome weapons as they climbed onto their dragons' backs. Once Oak was anchored in place, he attached his lance to the holding cord and placed his sword through the top of his leggings. The clan ascended into the canopies of the trees and they took great care their wings were only half extended.

As Thadities and Oak approached the uppermost treetops he watched as the tree limbs and their leaves moved as they glided past. Oak looked down and was astonished.

The whole of the wildwoods was dressed for battle. The forest floor was hidden underneath a thick and seething mist, and the wild and untamed trees stood in regimented lines. They looked forbidding. Jerome and a couple of his soldiers were just inside the western fringe of these trees and seemed to be having a lively discussion as defined by their hand movements. Oak heard nothing as he was too far away. The flight was short due to strong winds and they landed just as the sun fell over the edge of their homeland. Oak went to say hullo to Fielding and Thadities poked him in the back.

"Quiet Oak," whispered Thadities.

Oak went and stood at the edge of Thadities' talons and checked for his sword hilt. It was there. He'd been worried because he'd lost a sword twice over the last few weeks.

Forthwind came and stood next to him and checked her longbow and arrows. Oak placed his finger on his lips. Silence reigned.

Fielding nodded and said, "The navigators are a suspicious tribe. These are some of their odd beliefs.

"No navigator will sleep by the edge of a field in case they are paralysed in their sleep.

"Any navigator who cuts down trees near visiting places will also be paralysed.

"There is a graveyard near the north boundary, so trees must never be cut down from that holy place. It is said that genies live among those trees."

Fielding could not remember if there were any more, but the trees had kept these old wives' tales alive for centuries, and he was hopeful the navigators would be terrified out of their wits when they found some of their friends had disappeared.

"I am an ancient oak elder, and though I look exhausted and discouraged, I will fight until my last drop of sap is extinguished. The wildwoods must be saved; without the trees there would be no life. There is much evil afoot and we ancient trees cannot understand why they want to destroy the wildwoods for gold."

Adair and Shari soon joined them, exhausted, for their flight had been long and arduous. They sat on Thadities' nose and Adair said, "The navigators are camped in the centre of the star flower field and the poor flowers lie trampled underfoot. By their actions alone it shows they are an undisciplined unit, free men who plunder for the highest bidder."

Fielding looked pensive and then said, "Thadities, Oak please take care of Forthwind," as he looked at her with compassion.

Forthwind turned around and snapped that she would take care of herself and if Oak and Thadities needed a nursery maid, he could provide one. Nobody questioned her courage, and she was hurt. She'd never been asked for her opinion and this she accepted because she was unfamiliar with warfare, but she was no coward.

Everybody looked at her askance, but she was so angry she didn't care. She climbed back onto Grumpy and asked if she could be returned to camp.

Thadities and Oak bade goodnight to Fielding and they all left together. On their unexpected return to their camp they found it was not quite ready for habitation. Oak crawled close to Thadities and slept.

After a bit, Oak roused, watched Forthwind as she slept and wondered what had gone on in her head. He didn't know his sister at all, he thought. This melee would be a test for them both.

The sun rose, the camp emptied, and the dragons rose into a cold breeze. Oak wrapped his warm cloak around his body and wondered what the day would bring. The knots in his stomach unwound as they negotiated their way down into Fielding's clearing. The clearing was in an uproar. What had gone wrong now? Fielding and the wildwoods were very temperamental.

"The navigators are at the gates!" shouted Fielding. "It's now too late for you to be shown the root system, so the trees will be our eyes and ears."

Fielding looked at Thadities, and said, "I know your clan is well trained in the arts of trickery and evasion. After all, dragons and wildwoods are not mortal, we have a lot in common. Now is the time to show you our magic."

Fielding requested that Oak and Forthwind stand in front on his trunk. "Oak, Forthwind... I do beg your pardon for what I say when I talk about mortals. I am consumed by hatred and it has blighted my life. Your father and mother were protectors of the wildwoods and now you need to be courageous because you will battle your own kind. I hope you are victorious in defeating the navigators. Maybe we can then find peace."

Oak and Forthwind knelt and Fielding anointed their foreheads with his sap. They rose with tears glistening in their eyes.

The clan stayed behind with Fielding while Thadities and Oak stepped onto an unfamiliar pathway, and Oak felt alarmed with its dark and impenetrable foliage that lived amongst the dark shadows. He ran to keep up with Thadities' long legs.

"Agh!" he screeched, as one of the sentinel trees that lined the edge of the path bent down with its gnarled branch and tried to make a grab for his face. He knew he was barely tolerated by the independent trees, but didn't they realise he was trying to stop them from being felled?

Oak shifted and stood in front of Thadities and he watched the path make a sharp left turn. He made a grab for Thadities' leg, missed and they both fell heavily onto its surface. Oak scrambled for the edge of the path and clung on with the tips of his fingernails, as it wound its way around and around the bases of ancient trees. The wind spun his head around and Oak was finding it difficult to breathe, so he took shallow breaths until the path flung them both into a patch of hawthorn. The thorns pierced his skin and he watched his blood soak through his clothes, but no fear joined his blood. He looked over and found Thadities as solid as a rock, sitting amongst the thorns, grimacing.

Thadities and Oak re-joined the pathway and knew it was disgruntled by the way it had scattered a layer of debris over its surface, leaving the pathway obscured. Oak thought it was now getting very dangerous because they didn't know what was lurking underneath.

Then before Oak took another step the path gave a nasty little shake and Oak and Thadities lost their footing, were flung through the air and dropped onto the hard forest floor. They brushed themselves down and wearily climbed back onto the path without a word being spoken. Fielding had primed them about this rite of passage. If any chinks had shown in their armour of courage, the independents would have struck. They held no allegiance to any species and they detested men.

Oak watched in fascination as the centre of the pathway gave a malevolent stare before it retracted itself and snaked its way into the wildwoods. Permission was grudgingly bestowed for their safe passage to the edge of the wildwoods. An evil odour wafted under Oak's nose. He had not been forgiven.

Thadities placed his talon across his mouth to request Oak to be silent. They both watched the hedge, but Oak saw nothing and he wondered what Thadities saw.

And then he saw it too.

Hooks pierced the top limbs of the woven hedge and as the points dug into its heart, it howled. The leaves beat the navigators about their heads until they were forced to relinquish their hold and they disappeared from Oak's view. What next? he wondered as he moved closer to Thadities. He was lifted onto the dragon's back and they made it back to the clearing with no interference from the path, where they found Fielding had sprouted new roots from his trunk. In his limbs, Fielding held one of these tree roots, and it snaked its way back into the ground.

Forthwind came running up and said, "Fielding was told the navigators had surrounded the wildwoods and had attempted to batter them from all sides. They've been vanquished by the trees. Fielding asked us to observe the area from the sky and come up with some strategies to stop their continued bombardment of the trees."

The four of them took off into the tree canopies and conducted a reconnaissance. Oak and Thadities flew north west and Grumpy and Forthwind flew south west; between them the wildwoods were searched from one end to the other. Oak slipped and grabbed hold of the rope in shock, as he watched the navigators with their small cannons and iron balls. He had never seen such things but had heard tales brought back from over the seas by other knights and squires. They caused much damage and what could the trees use to defend themselves against these deadly cannons? He counted five and many hundreds of men. There were many more of them than he'd realised.

As they approached the tip of the wildwoods the navigators were more sparsely spaced and on the other side, no sign of them.

They met Grumpy and Forthwind on the return journey and they returned together to Fielding's clearing.

Once dismounted, he ran and fetched Forthwind and they both approached Fielding.

"What did you unearth on your reconnaissance, Forthwind?" Fielding enquired.

"Cannons, five in all, with piled iron balls placed behind them. They're placed about a few hundred yards apart on the south side of the wildwoods. Many navigators stood around these cannons and were gesturing wildly. I saw many more navigators but as we moved to the other side of the wildwoods, the men were more sparsely spaced."

Fielding fired back, "How many navigators?"

"Hundreds," she replied.

Fielding looked at Oak and asked for his observations. His answer was nearly the same. The navigators had a plan.

"Thadities," called Fielding. "I also have a plan."

The dragons followed a young sapling who scurried through a tunnel of hawthorn and there they waited with a curious air.

Thadities stepped forward with a quizzical look, which was soon replaced with a nod. He looked like a young warrior as he belched out his flame into the unresisting air. It died away and left a curl of black smoke in its wake.

Chalice followed. She hiked up her eyewear and opened her mouth. She nearly made it, just a few inches off, but it was enough to catch the hawthorn edge alight. She looked self-conscious.

Grumpy was up next, and Oak felt for him and wished with all his heart he would not be humiliated this morning. The last time he had been promoted to use his flame he had been embarrassed although he had managed to light the taper. Grumpy threw back his shoulder, flexed his wrinkly neck and roared. Out exploded a red and yellow flame and shot straight into the air. Oak clapped with glee and Grumpy winked in his direction.

Daffadilly, Waddle, and Steffen followed. They all stood tall and created vigorous flames which lit up the air above them.

Fielding had found his cannons.

Oak looked over the assembled clan and wondered how this could be and was filled with pride for them.

Thadities joined in the chat and congratulated them all for their commitment to the cause. The dragons looked to Grumpy and he said with pride, "Forthwind found an old recipe that offered a cure for flame revival. She found most of the herbs in the wildwoods with our help and brewed it to a consistency our tummies could tolerate. Waddle experimented first, and the metamorphosis was miraculous, so each one of us took a wooden spoonful. We have practised each day, in secret. Thadities; meet your rejuvenated warriors."

Oak stalked out of the clearing and didn't look back to see the hurt on the dragons' faces. He could keep a secret, so why wasn't he told?

Oak sulked and was ignored. His childishness was tolerated but Thadities was annoyed. Thadities decided to stop this childishness now.

"Oak," called Thadities.

Oak slouched over and glared at Thadities through lowered brows.

"Enough; the elementals need updated maps. Oak trees have gathered and shut out all but dappled light on the north west and north east borders of the wildwoods. The elementals and trolls want to know where to position their warriors for the wildwoods' best defence against the navigators. These same oaks have released scents that when inhaled mess with men's thoughts. I have spoken to Fielding regarding an antidote and this list of herbs must get to all our warriors. I have now decided that Forthwind will be my rider for this mission."

Oak was unable to stop his mouth from hanging down and he blinked back scalding tears. He didn't want to cry in front of them both, so he held them in tightly. He had caused enough trouble. What had he done?

Thadities and Forthwind were a speck in the sky by the time Oak moved from the spot he had been rooted to since that horrible blow had been delivered. As he moved, the whole clan found much to occupy them. He silently thanked them for their tolerance and decided his growth would start now. He started to walk towards Chalice, and as he looked up she had come to meet him half way. He ran and held onto her leg and sobbed. Her talon came down and rubbed his hair; this time no blood was drawn.

"Oak," she said softly, "go and fetch fresh water and food to last for a few days and then come and see me when you have finished."

Oak went and collected fresh water from the spring and found the freshest morsels of greens he could find for the dragons.

On his return he reported back to Chalice and asked, "What next?" He felt sick in the tummy, but he knew this too would pass.

The air shifted around them. Thadities and Forthwind had returned. Oak stood back and watched as Forthwind dismounted. She moved like a seasoned warrior, he thought, his sister; his rival, and now he must put his childishness aside and say sorry.

Thadities clapped his talons together and demanded their attention as he moved towards the council circle. Oak and Forthwind stood in the centre, friends again.

Thadities held up his talon for quiet and said, "there is a massive blockade in the north west of the wildwoods. Some ancient oak, elm, hawthorn, ash and birch are gathered there and have many supporters surrounding them. We were not welcome, and we left quickly."

As they landed near Fielding's clearing, Oak thought he looked a little ragged around the edges of his trunk, but he knew better than to mention his appearance. Fielding was known to be vain.

Oak watched Fielding have a temper spat as he grasped what had be going on in that part of the wildwoods. He gestured so hard he dislodged part of his root system which in turn caused more disruption. The attached soil worked its way loose and jumped back into its vacated holes.

"Fielding," said Thadities. "Calm yourself or you will do yourself some irreparable damage."

Fielding said, "These ancient inhabitants of the wildwoods have several demands they insist be met before they take up arms against the navigators. The main point is as follows: The hypocrisy of tyrants has devastated our way of life for thousands of years and we are worn out and ready to perish for our convictions. Men, in their stubbornness will soon be wiped off the face of the homelands. We will not take up arms."

Thadities grimaced and asked who they were.

"The Reformers," shouted Fielding.

Oak sidled up to Thadities and begged for his forgiveness. Thadities looked down and ruffled his hair. He had been forgiven. His small world had righted itself.

Fielding sent a message deep into his root system and they trawled underground until they had flushed out every tree, bush, flower, and blade of grass, urging them to ignore the demands of the Reformers.

A wave of ear-shattering sound vibrated throughout the wildwoods. The trees moaned out loud, using their highest octaves to drown out their sorrow at being told to denounce the Reformers.

One of the ugliest trees Oak had ever seen asked for an audience. He bowed and shouted, "Fielding, if the wildwoods understand our ancient history correctly, the Reformers have laid down not only our founding laws, which are supposed to have existed before the advent of man, and now they are told they are tyrants and to be expelled from the wildwoods. What has brought about this unheard-of anarchy? Why have you allowed those dragons," he stopped and pointed at Thadities and then continued, "to weave themselves into your soul?"

Fielding was not Lord Chancellor for nothing. He drew himself up to his full height and spoke above a whisper, calling the council of war to gather before the light crossed over into the darkness.

Chapter

# SEVENTEEN

Oak was overawed; all was ready for the council of war to begin. Gathered around Fielding were the chosen mouthpieces of the wildwoods and other clans. Thadities stood next to Chalice, and Oak next to Forthwind. The tree that had confronted Fielding earlier stood beyond her and so on until lastly a young sapling stood next to Thadities. Nobody was introduced.

Fielding spoke with fire. "I am fighting for our very survival. Don't you have any understanding of the evil the navigators have brought onto our homeland? The wildwoods are unable to fight in a chivalrous manner and need warriors who are capable of heroic deeds without losing their ability to be rational when it comes to the kill. I tricked Thadities into coming to Welddpool and then I begged until I received Thadities' pledge that he will defend the wildwoods. I am ashamed of my dishonourable conduct, but I had no recourse but the one I took."

Fielding took a deep breath and shouted, "I am angry with the Reformers because they've tried to sabotage my battle plans. I and parts of the wildwoods are primed for battle and now they have come along, out of nowhere, and poked their unwanted limbs into my affairs. That is why I want them to be expelled. I don't want the wildwoods to perish. There are a lot of good men on the homeland, and I know that one day the trees and men will have a greater understanding of their differences. It started with Oak's and Forthwind's father Rave; now they will teach their children, and their children's children through the generations until peace and harmony is their way of life."

Somebody shouted, "Are you pacifists?"

"No," replied Fielding.

Some believed they could crush the navigators' push for dominance, which in turn would leave them with many prisoners, and that would be another headache for another day. The collective was determined to diminish mans' hold on their wildwoods, and with no desire to perish, their chosen pathway would be to – fight. Each species had a vote. It was a unanimous - yes.

Fielding had the unenviable job to cut the Reformers and their roots from the collective. This would be done quietly.

Chapter

# EIGHTEEN

Oak woke and knew in his bones that something fiendish had been released into the shadowy, secretive wildwoods. A seething mass of malevolent hatred arose, and his homeland greeted it with silence.

Thadities woke and placed his talon against Oak's lips. The dragons and Forthwind were tired from last night's flight sequencing. During this flight they had, by eye, sectioned the wildwoods and had drawn simple maps; now they would know where each member of the clan each would at all times. This would be crucial to their defence and in keeping each other safe.

They tiptoed out of camp and rose as one into the new dawn. Oak looked down into the heart of the wildwoods and saw ancient trees had been uprooted from the earth and were leaning against their neighbours, as if looking for support. Why? Oak wondered.

Thadities came down into the clearing and spoke even before his talons had hit the forest floor. "What's happened? There is a pervading undercurrent that traverses the wildwoods and has seeped into the surrounding realm."

Oak said, "I felt it in my bones."

He was ignored, and Fielding spoke with a self-assurance that had been missed over the last few days. "The wildwoods are ready for battle. Adair joined me just as the sun rose and Shari was charged with the safety of her kinsfolk, the cavern and the delivering of any herbal remedies. She has also put a special guard in the library, and if the navigators reach there Rave's journal will be destroyed. The crystals have been generated and will be the force behind the root system. The collective's strategy is for every species in the wildwoods and beyond, to be now connected during the infestation of the navigators."

Thadities jumped up into the air and Oak saw that Adair had plonked himself down onto his nose. He had approached so silently neither had heard him.

"Vortex," said Adair in a whisper as he pointed the way.

"Adair, why did you whisper?" asked Thadities.

Adair replied, "I don't want to be overheard."

Thadities and Oak grinned. Adair was quietly spoken and difficult to hear most times and when he whispered it was very difficult to understand him.

The three of them grinned like fools. Adair's grin was infectious. He wiggled down into his harness and then Thadities nodded to Fielding and left the clearing. He walked with his wings pinned to his sides and at other times he skipped with wings flexed. Oak was not so afraid by the time they arrived at the vortex. Thadities had given him something else to think about and his thoughts had been engaged elsewhere.

He had never returned to the vortex since the last terrifying time when he had been made its captive.

Adair introduced them to the hawthorn trees which stood guard each side of the spiral. After much talk and hand gestures, Oak saw that Thadities had grasped the simple commands on how it was to be operated. The cooperation of the hawthorn trees was imperative for Thadities to be able to use the vortex and while they shook talon and limb Oak clapped his hands together in relief.

Chapter

# NINETEEN

Oak and Thadities returned to camp and found it in a hive of activity. Chalice said, "In your absence, Fielding asked we be moved closer to the centre of the wildwoods."

Oak took one last look around and they were off. Their wings battered the breeze, the leaves moved in tandem and they become one with the wildwoods. Accepted.

As soon as they arrived, Waddle set up camp with the help of the clan. When their assistance was no longer needed, Oak and Forthwind searched amongst the trees for a suitable place to hide. They soon chose a thick stand of ash trees that had huge limbs that were well hidden from prying eyes but which hung over one of the main pathways. They would be the first of the clan the navigators would encounter if they penetrated this far into the wildwoods.

They hid their spare weapons amongst the leaves and then returned to camp to find Daffadilly waiting for them with her grass plait clutched in her talon.

"These plaits, that keep our eyewear in place, have worn in places," she said.

Oak and Forthwind collected new grasses to replace the old ones. Their old shawls were now used as blankets since the last crossing over, and Grumpy's ear trumpet had been replaced by Forthwind's voice. She had an excellent pair of lungs. Oak could testify to that. After the repairs had been completed, Oak and Forthwind bade the dragons farewell and went to take up their posts.

The dragons watched them leave with a troubled look.

Oak and Forthwind were on the brink of honouring their homeland and its original inhabitants and the dragons would not smother them.

Oak and Forthwind were draped around two huge limbs and they peered through the silent leaves waiting for any navigators to appear.

"Tap, tap..." Oak heard the neighbouring tree tap his tree trunk. The navigators had made it this far without being stopped.

Oak whispered to Forthwind, "Are you ready?"

She whispered back, "Are you scared, Oak?"

"Yes, I have always been sick in the stomach just before a battle, but once it's begun I'm fine. I don't run. How's your stomach?" asked Oak.

Before Forthwind could reply Oak heard the trees wailing from the direction of the hedge. He looked down and saw the pathway detach itself from its moorings and fling itself around this stand of trees. The navigators ran out of the wildwoods and they looked white and scared. They ran to the centre of the clearing and formed a circle, each with their backs to the centre. Swords were at the ready and Oak heard them breathing hard and saw sweat run down some of their brows as they circled under his tree limb. Their leader seemed terrified as the trees kept up their unholy racket and Oak sniggered into his hand while he watched some of the navigators wet their pants. They shuffled around and around, eyes glued for any movement from the pathway and the strange behaviour of the wildwoods.

Silence. Oak wondered what was worse; the noise or the silence. Nothing moved except the petrified navigators. They kept going around and around and eventually came to an abrupt halt and looked into the tree canopies. Oak watched Forthwind as she placed an arrow into her bow and took aim.

The wailing rose in pitch as her first navigator sank to the wildwoods floor. Her aim had been remarkable, Oak thought. The trees started to whisper and Forthwind shot an arrow into the air. Her second mark fell to the ground, silently this time.

Oak thought he had better start and the hapless navigator who had sought refuge under his tree fell to the ground when Oak's lance found his arm. They navigators ran every which way, but the wildwoods would not let them leave. They now belonged to the trees.

Without any warning Jerome and his soldiers appeared and collected the hapless navigators.

He picked them up as if they were reeds and called for Oak. Oak crawled across the limb and Jerome plucked him off. Jerome said to the trees on the opposite side of the clearing, "Bind them tight and stow them away in the canopies; we will be back for them."

The trees unwound their gnarled limbs and tightly wound them around the navigators until they looked like ancient mummies. Oak noted that their eyes were unfocused with fear. After the limbs had hidden them amongst their leaves the trees were silent.

Jerome said to Oak, "No more navigators will use this pathway today; these men were lost. Their main unit has been sent to the north western side of the wildwoods where Thadities and the clan are fighting. Collect your things, lads," he added as he nodded to Forthwind. "You can join him and fight at the south east side of the wildwoods."

Forthwind giggled. "I'm not a lad, it's me; Forthwind. You know I am a girl," she told Jerome.

He scratched his head in wonder; he had thought her a lad. "No castle women I ever met displayed such marksmanship," he said to Forthwind.

They both collected their weapons and got ready to follow Jerome and his soldiers to their new camp. Thadities arrived at the clearing with Grumpy just behind him and shouted, "Halt. Sorry Jerome, they must come now. We'll talk later about the prisoners."

Oak and Forthwind yelled in excitement and mounted their friends. How would he know about the prisoners and why would Thadities' heart beat so fast?

Chapter

# TWENTY

Oak bawled like a baby when he saw how the navigators had damaged Fielding. They had hacked at his roots, his trunk and only stopped when they had been unable to reach his top limbs. Fielding's sap ran down his trunk and pooled near his damaged roots. His sap would now to be used to make rubber balls for the elementals' catapults, which had been fetched from the caverns' armoury.

"Dry your tears Oak, I will survive. Over the years I have sustained worse injuries and healed," said Fielding. "Now, Thadities, some of the navigators were hurt during the skirmish and all were taken prisoners. All prisoners need to be expelled from the wildwoods."

Oak remounted Thadities and he felt the dragon's anger jump under his skin. Oak kept quiet until they reached the vortex. He dismounted and watched. The trees released the navigators and then they were tossed from tree limb to tree limb with little ceremony until they all reached the hawthorn bushes. Unable to stand due to their injuries they were just piled up in an uneven heap and left to worry.

Thadities roared. He could be heard all over the wildwoods and the roots started to beat a tattoo from one tree to another. What was happening?

The hawthorn trees roots glowed and before Oak could ask any questions Grumpy and Forthwind arrived.

"Fielding has sent me, Thadities," said Grumpy. "Do you lack fire?"

"No, Grumpy, but two flames are stronger than one," Thadities replied.

The hawthorn bushes pulled apart their lower branches and a yawning cavity took their place. The navigators started to scream and finding some inner strength, tried to run. They were swiftly shut down and thrown into the cavity. They begged for mercy.

"The same mercy they have shown the wildwoods," shouted Thadities.

Oak realised then that the navigators had never before seen dragons. They were terrified and cowered into the back of the cavity. Grumpy and Thadities stood in front of the cavity and roared. Their red and yellow flame shot out of their mouths, and licked the sides of the vortex, which in turn created a spiral of hot air. They watched as it swirled around the navigators, picked them up and shot them upwards towards the open sky. Oak knew the vortex meant death to the navigators, and he knew he and Thadities had been lucky to have survived the experience. The hapless navigators would not.

Within a short time, the vortex was shut down, the hawthorn trees snaked across the entrance and they were ready to depart.

On returning to Fielding they found Adair helping with Fielding's wounds and after a few words they returned to camp.

Thadities called a council meeting. Oak and Forthwind stood in the centre and the dragons formed a circle around them; just like old times Oak thought. The tall trees stood around them and watched.

Tomorrow they would clash with the largest unit of the navigators. Guards would be posted by the wildwoods while they slept. Armour would be left on and their weapons close to hand. Every member of the clan would fight.

"That includes you, Waddle," Thadities said. "You and Daffadilly will fight alongside Grumpy and Forthwind. Chalice and Steffen will fight alongside Oak and me. You are hardened warriors now and I expect you to show much courage. I know you will not let me down."

The clan turned in early, and Oak slept with one eye open, propped up against Thadities, and watched the trees watching him. Just before the sun rose, a thick mist curled its way around the wildwoods. It covered every nook and crevice, and then lay dormant. When Oak stood in the middle of the murk it came up to his knees. It felt nasty. The nervous tension it brought with it made everyone jumpy in the camp.

Thadities told them to ignore it and get on with their morning jobs. It was Oak's turn to fetch their morning meal, and as he walked towards Waddle he noticed the thick mist had thinned and he saw the forest floor beneath his boots. On his return with the food the mist, once again, thinned until he reached the clearing. The mist thickened while he and Forthwind ate.

"It's alive," Oak shouted to Forthwind.

"Don't be stupid," said Forthwind. "How can a mist be alive?"

"Well it is," insisted Oak.

The yelling brought Thadities down from the top of their camp and he asked, "What's going on here? You can be heard yelling all over the wildwoods and quiet is demanded from the clans."

Oak explained about the mist and Thadities said, "No, the mist is caused by warmer water being in the air and it was quickly cooled by the cold land when it paid it a visit. The wildwoods will manipulate these conditions until the mist disappears. It is not alive, sorry Oak."

Oak grudgingly apologised to Forthwind and they were friends once again. Thadities would not tolerate anger and disobedience from those who served under him. He said such things got others killed.

The mist shifted, the leaves crackled as if in response, and Oak fell to the ground. Unhurt, he picked himself up and knew that something had happened. The wildwoods had metamorphosed, and Oak was afraid. He looked over to the camp and saw that everyone had got to their feet and were brushing themselves down.

Thadities called for a meeting and said they would all cross over into Fielding's clearing and find out what had just happened.

They entered the clearing and Oak saw that Fielding looked better today and told him so.

"Thadities, thank the saints you are here!" He smiled at Oak. "The wildwoods have changed some of our strategies for the coming clashes. We have gathered new knowledge about the strength of the navigators, and we set new snares. The roots have delivered these strategies and now the wildwoods are ready for the next onslaught. You and the clan will just have to muddle along the best you can, sorry. I'm delighted to know the shift affected you; when time shifts back you will know."

Thadities replied with an alarmed frown distorting his usually placid face. "I'm bewildered by the sinister necromancy which you have forged throughout these wildwoods. We dragons are novices compared to the trees."

"You're not novices. If you'd been novices and outsiders, we would have never manipulated you to come to Welddpool and you would never ever have crossed the hedge and stepped one talon into the wildwoods. You are excellent warriors and while the wildwoods are still being invaded we need your continued help," replied Fielding.

Oak found himself once again thrown to the forest floor. He thanked the saints they were all unhurt, and he was miffed with the uncontrolled wildwoods.

Oak went over to Thadities and before he had marshalled his thoughts, he caught the last of their conversation. Ah, thought Oak, it was all for a reason. Better not cause any more trouble, he was in enough trouble already for making a noise.

Darkness descended from nowhere and Oak went and stood under Thadities' body and shook. "What's happened, Thadities?" Oak whispered.

"Stay here; don't move until I return," shouted Thadities, and he was soon lost to the darkness beyond.

Oak heard Fielding and Thadities talking in a muffled whisper, the darkness parted and Thadities reappeared, and they walked the few steps back to camp.

Chapter

# TWENTY-ONE

Oak felt Forthwind's fingers as she traced his face.

"What's the matter, Forthwind?" cried out Oak. "Are you frightened of the dark?

"I've lost my sight, Oak," screamed Forthwind.

"Breathe and calm down, Forthwind," said Oak, as he pulled her towards him.

Oak watched as her eyes opened and tears started rolling down her cheeks.

"Oh Oak, I thought I couldn't see. I had my eyes shut while practising with my bow and when I opened them darkness had descended. What a silly mistake."

Oak replied, "Not silly, we've been exposed to so many unfathomable and wondrous experiences since the start of the quest, it's been difficult for both of us. It was also very frightening when Thadities and the dragons found it all unfathomable as well. After all, they're the wise ones."

They stayed huddled together until Thadities re-joined them. "Oak and Forthwind, climb aboard. The navigators have entered the wildwoods with their fire cannons. Jerome kept them at bay as long as he could, but they destroyed the hedge in several places with their iron balls."

They met at the clearing. Thadities and the clan caught an unexpected upward draught and Oak was surprised, until he saw two huge oak trees, which sat on either side of the clearing, swirling their limbs around making a friendly wind spiral. They were on their way.

The canopies showed Thadities the best way to the encounter. They turned their leaves inside out to mark the way. Oak got better at noticing the different shades of the leaves and was thankful the clan was behind them; they would have no idea where to land. Oak watched a couple of tree canopies part up ahead, and Thadities and the other dragons were shown where they could descend. Thadities was an expert; he folded his wings closer to his body and descended on the forest floor without a scratch. The clan followed but Chalice snagged her wing on a tree limb and though she tried to not cry out, she squealed into her chest.

Forthwind ran over to check she was not too hurt and gave her a squeeze. Within minutes she was soaked to the skin. Chalice had cried, silently, and the tears had caught her unawares. Forthwind didn't say a word, her secret was safe with her.

The dragons formed a line behind Thadities and stopped when a snap was heard from somewhere in the wildwoods. Next, Oak heard a scuffle and when he turned around, he looked straight into the eyes of the navigators who stood on the pathway behind him. Grumpy moved slightly to his right and coughed. Out poured a red and yellow flame that caught the dry grass in the centre of the pathway and formed a ring of fire. The pathway shifted, and the navigators looked as if they had been turned to stone with fear. The fire spread farther down the centre of the pathway and was lost in the undergrowth; not a black singe was to be seen where the fire had burnt.

Oak looked at Thadities and asked, "What magic is this?"

"Shush Oak," said Thadities, as he placed a talon over his lips.

Thadities looked down at the navigators, bent his neck and plucked up a terrified navigator with his teeth. The hapless navigator swung back and forth in front of Oak's eyes and Oak watched in horror as the navigator slipped his arms out of his shirt and screamed until he hit the ground. Oak watched Thadities as he spat out the cloth which still clung to his mouth. He had made no attempt to pluck the man out of the air to stop his fall. Oak thought he'd been very lucky that Thadities had plucked him out of the air the time he had fallen.

He wound his arms around the dragon's neck and gave him a quick squeeze.

Oak looked down at the ground and noticed the flame had not diminished since it had been lit. The navigators had not moved, and their panic-stricken gaze was fastened onto the licking red and yellow flames and beyond. Oak realised that beyond stood the dragons and Jerome hidden between the suffocating darkness and the flames. It must seem to them that an ancient myth had come alive and the wildwoods were an even scarier place to be than they had imagined when they had listened to the myths and old wives' tales.

Thadities, the dragons, Oak, Forthwind and Jerome all stood around, scratched their heads and wondered where the next skirmish would come from. Apart from the fire ring the wildwoods were still in semi darkness. They had caught the navigators unawares because they had blundered onto the pathway in the darkness, and the pathway had decided to scare them to death, by throwing them around the wildwoods and into the clutches of the clan. They had seen the fear flow out of their eyes when they had been taken.

Thadities looked towards Jerome and said, "Isn't this the strangest skirmish? We're expected to know our boundaries, without ever being forewarned which part of the wildwoods is engaged in isolated skirmishes with the navigators. The root system isn't co-operating with us at present and the sovereigns of the wildwoods have shut us out of their inner council. No strategic plots have been given to us and we have so few of their own. We've never seen a cannon or their iron balls before in our lives. As aliens we are not privy to their strategies and so we can fight independently of them. Maybe that is why we are so useful to them. The navigators don't know we are here." Thadities shrugged and moved closer to Jerome.

Jerome acquiesced and then said to Forthwind and Oak, "Be courageous and follow me to the hedge. Thadities and the clan need time to think about the problem of the canons and their iron balls. If the iron balls found their mark, the dragons could be killed or at least maimed for life."

Oak wanted to say he and Forthwind would be killed just as quickly, but as he glanced towards Jerome's troubled face, he decided to shut his mouth and say nothing.

Oak and Forthwind held their weapons close to their bodies and followed Jerome onto the pathway. The pathway contained the fire to a straight and narrow line that travelled right in its centre, and only singed the ground beneath it. Oak breathed a sigh of relief. He thought he might be burnt alive because Grumpy had only lit the fire ring and not this continual magical line of flame.

Oak and Forthwind stepped onto the pathway and waited. The pathway never moved; instead it wound around the base of the ancient trees and Oak was able to distinguish the different species as they sped past. The trees were not being obnoxious today and allowed them to pass without any interference. Oak was an old hand now in his dealings with the wildwoods, and he knew they were being watched the whole time. When they saw the woven hedge, he was even more surprised that it gave them full protection to watch the navigators from a distance.

The darkness had started to lighten on their journey to the hedge, and by the time they arrived it had brightened to a slight haze. The air shimmered around Oak and he looked to the skies for the dragons, but the sky was empty. Oak threw his hand into the air. It brushed past some leaves, but otherwise there was nothing there, only a sensation of the air being heavier than usual. Wisdom he had obtained during the flights with the dragons had taught him the difference about air thicknesses and there was something odd about the air today, he thought. It felt like treacle.

Oak looked over to the hedge and there stood the brazen navigators with no protection, except their cannons and iron balls. They stood dotted around the field in groups of three. Oak, Forthwind and Jerome watched them with curiosity because they had never seen cannons before, let alone seeing one fire its iron ball.

Soon one navigator placed the iron ball into its gaping mouth, one poured white powder into the other end of the tube and yet another poked the powder with a stick. Odd, Oak thought, but he knew that somehow when those black tubes were lit, they could send those lethal iron balls over the hedge and into the wildwoods beyond. A shout was heard in the distance and the navigators all turned and looked towards the first cannon. A fire stick was held at the back of the tube and it roared. The navigator was thrown to the ground.

The iron ball whizzed past Oak's and Forthwind's heads. It crashed somewhere in the wildwoods behind them, but only silence greeted that ball.

The navigators were watched by three pair of eyes as they set another cannon to face a stand of trees farther along the wildwoods fringe. Oak looked at Jerome in fear, but he placed his thick finger against his mouth and hushed him.

Bang! went the next iron ball and Oak shook as it hit the centre of an isolated tree stand. The crying and creaking could be heard all over the wildwoods. "The navigators shouldn't have done that," Oak said to Forthwind in a whisper.

The navigators kept up their attack until all the cannons had been emptied. The wildwoods had greeted each iron ball with either silence or distress.

Oak noticed that Forthwind's arrow was rested on her longbow. She smiled at Oak and nudged him to be ready for the forthcoming clash. Oak showed her he was ready; he had his sword and lance right next to him, leant up against an obliging tree.

Oak was unable to see or breathe well; the air had turned heavy and it sat on his chest. He fought down the rising panic and waited for Jerome and Forthwind to move. The air shifted, and Oak followed close behind. He banged into Forthwind and watched as she bent down, placed an arrow into her longbow and shot. She continued shooting into the haze; her arrows found the hapless navigators because they had nowhere to run. Their cannons were also silenced by the descending mist.

Oak felt like the odd squire out. Forthwind was a formidable opponent and courageous for a lady's maid, but his mastery over his weapons had been wasted since this skirmish had started. Why had the dragons come to his homeland and looked for a knight if they were not going to use his services?

Oak turned around when he saw his sleeve flutter. Thadities had glided down onto the wildwoods floor and had not made a sound. He bent his neck, and Oak climbed upwards until his fingertips found the indentation. He held his sword aloft in one hand and with his other scrabbled for the cord. He lowered his head into the oncoming wind and held on for dear life. He could barely breathe, but his hold didn't slacken until Thadities landed. He slid down and was ready to move when Thadities tapped him on his shoulder.

The thick air cushioned their footfalls as they strode towards the pandemonium just up ahead. Oak heard the navigators screech like squealing pigs and he wondered who had hit a target.

The clan stood side by side behind the navigators' farthest lines. Oak glanced across either side of him and thought that Thadities and the dragons looked majestic. Their skin glowed through the wet mist and their flames were glorious as they checked one another's fire.

As he watched the mist evaporate, he saw the bright orb of the sun shine down from the sky, lighting up the dragons' skin even further and they still waited for the navigators to turn around and realise they were not alone.

Oak watched the colour bleed from the navigators' skins when they eventually turned around. They stood rooted to the spot and some were bending over as if they vomited. Oak remembered very well his first reaction to the dragons; it was not a pleasant memory to recall.

"Oak,' Thadities called softly. "The navigator that stands with the lighted stick needs to be stopped."

Oak held his sword aloft and ran towards the navigator. His sword held high, he whacked the lighted stick out of the navigator's hand and it spun out of control. It dropped onto the dry grass and it soon caught alight. The man moved quicker than Oak foresaw, but as he lunged towards the sword, Oak was able to sidestep and he missed. He made a second grab for Oak's sword, but Oak held on while the navigator, with a downwards shift of his hand, opened his skin and the blood squirted everywhere. Oak looked into his eyes and saw horror lurking there; he fell to the ground and was quiet.

Oak returned to Thadities' side and grinned.

Some of the navigators had run towards the barrier but others found some courage lurking in their breasts and had stood their ground. They then ran towards the cannons and tried to shove the iron balls into the back tubes. One cannon was lit quickly, and the iron ball sailed through the air on a direct path to Jerome. He stood still, and with his lethal club searched for the iron ball. A loud crack vibrated around the wildwoods when the club met the ball. It sailed back over the barrier and exploded on impact. The clan watched as the ball skidded into a loose pile of iron balls and caused a huge eruption. After the smoke wafted away, a black hole appeared where the pile of iron balls had been stored.

Thadities stood on his hind legs and scanned the field. Out of his mouth dribbled a thin blue and yellow flame, and as it wafted through the breeze it took on a life of its own. It manifested into the largest fire storm Oak had ever witnessed. It roared towards the nearest navigators and their cannon, and all that was left to see was a black singe mark on the ground where they had stood. The flame had not singed another blade of grass.

Oak looked towards the wildwoods and watched the navigators disappear into its depths. The hedge's limbs had earlier drawn apart and now allowed them to enter the wildwoods unhindered. The terrified navigators stampeded through without a thought to what lay ahead of them.

Forthwind ran out of the wildwoods and mounted Grumpy. Oak remounted Thadities and the two dragons walked together along the edge of the wildwoods and sought deserters.

Daffadilly, Waddle and Steffen were left behind to fire storm the remainder of the cannons. Oak watched Steffen as he shot his yellow and red flame into the air. It arched and caught the unattended cannon on the other side. He lost sight of them then, but he heard their continued roars as they destroyed the cannons and the iron balls. They had never used such nasty weapons and Daffadilly confided in Oak later that the dragons felt chivalry was going to the dogs. Oak hoped not.

By midday they had all returned to Fielding's clearing, tired but elated. Before they spoke they were shushed by Fielding as he continued listening to the roots. Fielding then bade them welcome and told them that the roots had watched a few stragglers enter the clearing and that they now stood near the vortex.

Fielding laughed as he related the story as told by the roots. "They stepped upon the outside pathway and when they were settled it tore itself up from the ground and wove through the wildwoods. All the while the navigators just hung on with their fingertips. When the pathway had had enough it flung them to the ground. Some banged their heads, others broke bones and even more were terrorised out of their wits. Most are now bound in the tree canopies with one or two on the loose. These loose stragglers are now near the vortex."

"Oak, Forthwind," Fielding continued. "The roots know where they are being held and the main pathway with the centre flame will guide you to them."

Oak and Forthwind stepped onto the outside of the pathway and kept away from the centre flame. It still burnt with a force Oak was unable to understand but he followed the pathway as it led them through the wildwoods to where the hapless navigators were waiting.

Forthwind spoke to them as they cowered amongst the leaves. "My name is Forthwind. Can I be of any help?"

The trees gave their quarry into Oak and Forthwind's capable hands and the navigators came down, eyes shining when they alighted upon Forthwind's beautiful face. They tried to explain, all at once, that they were hurt and hungry and they asked was there anywhere where they could get a drink? Forthwind beckoned them to follow her and they did without a qualm. On reaching the vortex, she showed them her longbow and Oak stood brandishing his sword. Defeated, they went meekly into the vortex and joined the other stragglers who were waiting there, a broken and dispirited group of men. One stopped at the entrance and tried to run but Forthwind shot an arrow into his foot, and he soon rejoined his fellow navigators. They were last seen being drawn up into the cruel spiral of wind, screaming all the way.

Oak and Forthwind joined the pathway once more and had an uneventful journey back to the clearing.

There, Oak almost jumped out of his skin. The noise from the centre of the wildwoods was intense. It blocked his ears and he was deaf to all sounds. He learnt later it was deliberate; he and Forthwind were not to be privy to that conversation.

He stood by and waited in a fog of silence. He was beckoned over, and he remounted Thadities. They left the clearing with Grumpy and Forthwind close behind. They mounted a higher pathway and were carried along a few feet off the ground. Oak knew then, with some certainty, they were still only being tolerated because of Fielding. Thadities had listed a little to the right and he was pushed back quite roughly to the middle of the pathway. This unfriendly behaviour continued until they reached the most beautiful place Oak had ever seen. It was a huge cleared circle drenched in sunlight. Stands of tall trees with straight trunks and different coloured leaves glowed through a fine mist that clung to their surface. Oak breathed in the mist and slipped towards Thadities' neck because he couldn't sit upright.

Chapter

# TWENTY-TWO

Oak woke to a warm breeze flitting past and his mind snapped back to the present. What had happened? He looked towards Forthwind and she seemed to have had the same reaction to this magical place.

One of the largest trees bade them over with its lower limbs and spoke. "Fielding has sent you and the clan to help us. This place is called an arboretum, and this is where the ancient elders gathered when the wildwoods were in danger. You have earned the respect that will be shown to the clan during this gathering. The circle is charmed, and you must take care that the imps that live amongst the trees don't play too many naughty tricks." The tree crackled.

The ancient one then clapped his limbs and out from behind the leaves came Adair and Shari; they were the imps.

It was so good to see them both again and there was much laughter and many hugs.

"A few surviving navigators must return home with no memories of the wildwoods. They will be herded into a clearing for their memories to be erased by a special potion that has been prepared by the elementals this daybreak and the dragons are asked to fly them back to their galleons."

The tree continued, "Tree bark that has great worth and some of our rarer plants are to be found only here. They are precious because they contain magical qualities to help heal many kinsfolk. This part of the wildwoods will be shut down from the outside world because now there is only greed and a lack of understanding of the truth of the way we and the other plants co-exist.

"The navigators have searched many faraway lands, and the council has learnt that a great burn takes place after they have cut down most of the trees, pulled out all the plants, herbs and fungi and then they are stored in the bowels of their galleons to be sold to the highest bidder. Around sixty trees are used to build one galleon which is why so many trees are destroyed. Much gold is being offered for this sacrilege.

"When kings, queens and high-born men are sick, they send for their herbalists. They are now listening to the tales that there are rare herbs to be found in some far-off lands that can prolong their lives for many years. Therefore, it is even more crucial that this small part of the wildwoods be shut down until Oak's and Forthwind's descendants are ready to receive the keys to unlock the secrets of herbal lore."

Oak watched tears drop from Thadities' eyes and marvelled how such a magnificent beast could have such a soft heart.

The trees at the edge of the clearing moved to allow the ones shielded behind to step forward. These species of trees look different, Oak thought. They were the ancient trees' guards. Oak felt the power radiate from them and he gave a prayer to his saints that they were fighting the same foe.

They left the arboretum and Oak felt quite lost for a few moments. He wanted to go back and sink into the magic. Thadities turned his neck and plucked him up by his shirt and shook him until his teeth rattled. He was soon himself and found himself once more standing in front of Fielding.

Jerome, Thadities and the clan left together after checking all their armour and weaponry. They stepped onto a very pleasant pathway. It allowed them to walk two abreast and converse without any interference. Even the trees showed tranquil faces while the clan discussed their strategies for the next melee.

Thadities and the clan didn't make a sound while they watched for the navigators to appear. Oak heard his heartbeat echoing in his ears, but it was a courageous beat and not one of a coward.

Oak watched the leaves shift as the tree roots slithered along the ground and disappeared into the soil, then he caught the slightest sound that came from somewhere behind him. The sound strengthened until it became a high-pitched scream coming from somewhere under Oak's feet. Then the thump of the navigators' boots joined the chorale as they came towards them. One by one the trees stopped their screaming and stood and waited with the clan. The footsteps faltered every so often and Oak wondered if the wildwoods were making their progress difficult.

Soon after this thought they appeared and they looked a motley lot now. They had been frightened out of their wits by the loss of their cannons and by having seen the dragons and a troll that very morning. The surrounding trees started to pelt them with their nuts. They pulled back their limbs, flung them forward and hundreds of nuts were released. Many found their targets and the navigators stuck their hands over their heads for protection and started to run. They ran towards the opposite edge of the wildwoods from whence they come. Oak wondered why they don't feel the sting of the nuts as they followed at a distance.

A bright light appeared from the left-hand side of the woods and it was the flame from the magical pathway. The flame still consumed the air above it without harming anything around it. It continued its merry way, following the path the navigators had trodden. By the time the clan had reached the navigators they were beyond being reasoned with. Between the screaming of the trees, their lethal nuts and the brazen flame, the navigators were ready to surrender to the dragons.

It was soon over. They were rounded up by the dragons and were brought back to the vortex. Thadities and the hawthorn trees fed the navigators into the wind tunnel and after their first cries were heard it was followed by a deafening silence. It was over and because the dragons had scuttled all their row boats, the few navigators that were left would be taken by the dragons to their galleons so they could sail their ships back to their homelands with tall tales about their bravery and the barren wildwoods they left behind. If they remembered anything at all, the memories would sound like a fantasy tale.

After the few navigators were flown to their ships, Thadities and the clan returned to the arboretum and stood in front of the ancient elder. Thadities said, "We have come to say farewell."

The ancient tree beckoned to Oak and Forthwind, "Come closer."

Oak and Forthwind stood at the base of the old tree and was shown some lichen-covered stones. Oak bent down and pulled them aside to reveal a cache of seeds resting in a natural hollow deep under the earth. Forthwind peered over his shoulder and gasped at the hundreds of seeds gathered there.

The ancient one said, "Oak, Forthwind those seeds are your heritage. Every species is to be found amongst these seeds."

He continued to look at Oak and he said, "Every year on your birth day, you will enter the wildwoods. You will be watched by the trees and brought before me to check the seeds. If any seeds are sick, you will be shown where to collect healthy ones to replace them. Do you understand now why you were found by the dragons? As well as a knight of the realm, Oak, you will be a knight of the wildwoods.

"Forthwind, Oak will be called away to take part in tournaments, battles and quests. While he is away it will be your duty to attend to the seeds. Our wish is that this pattern will become part of your lives as you grow into adulthood and then be passed on to your young ones."

Oak was bemused but his heart thudded with excitement. He was to become a knight of the wildwoods.

Thadities came and stood in front of Oak and said he was to be knighted. Oak got down on his knees and waited. Thadities requested Oak's sword and placed it on his shoulder. His voice rang out as he made Oak a knight of the wildwoods.

Oak rose, and his skin glowed bright red. He then disgraced himself even more, by vomiting into his boots.

Forthwind, Jerome, Thadities and the clan just pretended nothing was amiss, and they crowded around and gave him their heartiest congratulations.

They said their farewells and returned to Fielding by a peaceful and subdued pathway. They entered the clearing to find Fielding had left without saying goodbye. It had gone where Thadities and the clan could not follow.

"Fielding," Oak yelled as he ran to hug his trunk, but there was no response.

"Oh, Thadities," cried Oak. "We weren't able to say goodbye. Fielding has blended back into the wildwoods and wears his cloak of silence and where are Adair and Shari?"

He ran to the cavern steps and pushed on the stone top. It was stuck. "Thadities," he called.

The dragons looked like statues, but he needed their help. He pointed towards the ancient stone. He was ignored, and he ran to the clan, frightened.

Oak went and hugged the dragons one by one, looked into their beautiful faces and said, "Sir Glyneath is a fair master and I look forward to your meeting with him."

Silence vibrated though the air.

Oak laughed and said, "I see I'm being ignored. Why is that, Thadities?"

Thadities ruffled his hair and said nothing.

Thadities shooed them both out of the clearing. Oak and Forthwind slowly walked towards the edge of the wildwoods, looking over their shoulders every now and then, checking if they were being followed by the dragons. Then they spied the sunlight pouring down with its enticing rays, beckoning Oak and Forthwind to come out and play. Oak grabbed Forthwind's hand and they both ran laughing into the sunlight.

The warm sun played with their skins and Oak turned and called the dragons to come and feel its warmth. They hadn't followed them out and they weren't there.

Oak dashed back to the hedge and peered into the gloom beyond. His eyes were not able to penetrate further than the first row of trees.

Oak called for Forthwind, "The woven hedge won't let me in. The dragons must be in trouble!"

Oak and Forthwind dashed down the edge of the wildwoods, and peered here and there, but nothing was to be seen through the dense darkness. Their friends had vanished!

Oak, with a sinking feeling in his stomach picked up his weapons and headed towards Pembrokeshire castle, Forthwind by his side. They walked, stumbled, cried and promised never to lose touch with one another.

Darkness was descending as they climbed one last hillock before they stepped onto the tournament field and Oak saw the tournament tents were gone. As they ran through the field towards the castle, muffled voices were heard, coming from behind the castle walls. Birds and butterflies flitted around their heads, and then Oak heard Sir Glyneath's voice as it bellowed over the wall, "Oak, where are you lad?

They ran towards Oak's master, knowing in their hearts, they would see one another on King's birth days and special holidays and the dragons would never be forgotten.

Printed in the United States
By Bookmasters